MAGNITUDE

T. N. Kaylor

Magnitude

This is a work of fiction. Names, characters, businesses, places, events and incidents are either the products of the author's imagination or used in a fictitious manner. Any resemblance to actual persons, living or dead, or actual events is purely coincidental.

Amazon print edition.
   ISBN-10:
   1-946948-06-3
   ISBN-13:
   978-1-946948-06-9

Amazon Kindle edition.
   ISBN-10:
   1-946948-07-1
   ISBN-13:
   978-1-946948-07-6

   Library of Congress Control Number: 2017904516
   Copyright © 2017 by T. N. Kaylor

Cover design by Gorify™.
Edited by Robert H. Kaylor

All rights reserved. Published in the United States by Gorify™.
www.tnkaylor.com

Dedicated to Trever, who helped me reclaim this story.

Thank you for being the leader of our creative tribe all these years.

1

Junkyard Overture

She should be dead.

A skeleton crew worked under flickering tungsten lights in the scrapyard as the sun dipped behind Mount Charleston. Cast in shades of blue, a three-ton grapple magnet swung on the end of the yellow crane that rolled toward her wrecked Subaru Forester. For the first time since her accident, the severity of the crash shook Dallas, and the shattered bone in her right arm ached as a reminder.

(I'm lucky.)

Always the engineer, she admired the way her external fixator screwed directly into her broken arm. Then a loud noise demanded her attention.

CLUNK.

The four-foot circular magnet stuck to her smashed car roof, and the retractable claws wrapped around the crumpled body like monster talons. Clanking pneumatic joints closed as the pincer punctured through the side doors and gripped the wreckage. The crane lifted her SUV, and it glided overhead with its loose muffler dangling.

A haunting image of a disemboweled body gliding overhead with hanging entrails flashed in her mind.

(Ramone.)

Dallas pushed back the horrible memory and focused on the junkyard.

(Stay here. Be in the now.)

The claw opened, and her Subaru landed in front of the crusher.

CRASH.

The suspension bounced. Tireless wheels kicked up a cloud of dust that drifted outward like spreading fog. Luca climbed out of the crane and joined Dallas. The Caterpillar 928F loader rammed the side of her Forester with forks that reminded her of the water hammer at Turbine No. 6 a month ago. The machine lifted her car and pushed it into the salvage crusher. Luca smoked his occult pipe.

(That pipe.)

"Too bad. Was good car." Luca's *W* sounded like a *V*. He had a cartoon vampire's accent. As he blew smoke, he handed her some motorcycle parts.

"It was," Dallas agreed, taking the carburetor and headlight and shoving them in her bag. "Thanks for your help."

The operator climbed down from the loader and pressed a green button on the gray control box of the E-Z Crusher. The heavy top plate slid downward on its pneumatic posts.

Whirrrrrrl.

The sound reminded Dallas of the box bailer she used while working at Home Depot during her freshman and sophomore years of college. The plate pressed into the roof of the Subaru and her car surrendered like cardboard. Mesmerized, Dallas watched the machine squeeze the SUV into a two-foot-high wad of metal and fiberglass. The operator pushed another button, and the crusher retracted.

Then he climbed back into the loader, slid his forks under the compacted rectangle that used to be her car, and drove it into a maze where he would add the block to a wall of smashed vehicles on the perimeter of the property.

"Paperwork?" Luca asked.

"Sure, let's wrap this up." Dallas followed Luca toward his office, a repurposed railroad caboose in front of the *Pick-A-Part*. They wove through the aisles of the vehicle graveyard, past a field of rusty posts that marked the future resting place of car carcasses. As they hiked toward the office, Dallas delighted in the changing colors of stacked, squashed auto bodies as night fell. The slants and tilts of the blocks made Dallas question their security. The great wall could tumble and crush them at any second.

(So vulnerable.)

"Have you worked here the whole time you've lived in Vegas?" Dallas asked, hoping to distract herself with chit chat.

"Yes. Since I come to America. Two years." Luca smiled. "I like."

"So you came from?" Dallas followed him. "Where exactly are you from, Luca?"

"Wallachia." He pronounced it *Va-lAke-i-a*.

They climbed the metal steps to the narrow entrance of the faded-red train car. She liked the sound of her boots.

Clang, clink, clang.

"And you came directly to Las Vegas from?" She knew she'd butcher the pronunciation of his home country, so she didn't try. "There?"

"Yes."

"I was born in Detroit," Dallas said.

Luca's expression told her that he didn't know where that was.

"It's cold there. In the middle, but North. Near Canada."

Still, the location did not register with Luca.

"My dad moved here for work. I've lived here most my life now. Sometimes I think I'd like to be anywhere else."

"Vegas nice," Luca said from inside, switching on the light. He offered his hand to help her inside, just like a gentleman in an old-time movie.

(Must be a European thing. Vegas guys are NOT like this.)

Politely, Dallas laughed as she took his hand and stepped into the caboose-office. "I have to disagree with you on that one, Luca. Vegas is pretty far from 'nice.'" Dallas had never been inside a caboose before. Luca had converted the tiny square room into a dumpy, but functional, administrative workspace. Dallas poked around the cluttered office.

(What a creative use of obsolete resources.)

"Vegas can be downright nasty. In so many ways," she said.

"How you mean 'nasty?'" Luca asked, resting his spent pipe in a filthy ashtray.

"Let's just say locals are 'nice' as long as they keep getting tipped. Beyond that, they'd rather slit your throat than talk to you." Dallas eyed the room more carefully. Antique license plates covered the walls from floor to ceiling. She traced the rusty letter V on a dark yellow tag from Alaska. Other rusty signs for motor oil and Micheline tires layered the wall. Old pinup calendar pics hung here and there. Dallas threw her messenger bag onto a torn swivel chair with a missing back. Luca shuffled through a stack of papers on a circa 1960 metal desk until he found the invoice for Dallas. He handed her an old chewed up Bic.

"Read." He pointed at different places on the triplicate form. "Sign."

While Dallas reviewed the salvage claim, Luca tidied the hyper-masculine reception area. He stacked *Maxim* and *Car and Motor* magazines on a rickety wooden coffee table. After gathering two fistfuls of stained coffee mugs, Luca swung by the door to peek out the window and then set the dirty dishes in a tiny sink in the opposite corner. Back at the desk, he handed Dallas her bag. "I done for day. You need ride home?"

Getting better with her injured arm, Dallas scribbled her signature on the bottom line, took her bag from Luca, and slung it across her body. "Makes sense, since we're neighbors. I haven't had a chance to car shop yet. I had to take a cab here. Next time, I'll be sure to get the rental reimbursement option on my auto insurance."

"Rent re-burse?"

"So they pay for a rental car. I've been bumming rides and hailing taxis for a month now."

Luca made an *after-you* gesture toward the door, and Dallas went to exit. He followed. The knob didn't budge when she twisted it. Then Luca switched off the light behind her. He stood too close.

"You lovely woman for a black."

Dallas looked over her shoulder as he moved in on her. "What?"

"I say. You lovely." Luca caressed her cheek with the back of his hand.

"Let me go!"

"Why hurry?"

"Unlock this door, Luca!" Dallas yelled as she frantically rattled the doorknob.

(No button lock. Only a keyhole.)

Even though he stood shorter than her, Luca backed her up against the wall. He clenched her biceps and pinned them against the door at her sides.

(He's strong.)

She pulled away. But Luca buried his face in her chest instead of moving in for the kiss. Dallas wriggled and writhed as he pressed against her. The license plates rattled against the walls, making the room tremble. Sucking a huge breath, she rammed her knee into Luca's crotch. Dallas slid aside as Luca toppled into a pile in front of the door.

"Curve!" Luca cursed as he curled up in agony, grabbing his balls.

Dallas darted down the dark hall into the length of the caboose, hoping to find another door on the backend. She made it to the last room with Luca on her tail. Street light shined through tiny windows, casting patches of yellow throughout the darkness. On her left, a small fold-out table with a booth sat covered with tattered porno magazines. On the right, bunk beds attached to the wall. On the floor, wadded stained sheets and a wool blanket blocked the door. Dallas lunged for the doorknob and twisted it. It opened an inch when Luca grabbed a fistful of Dallas's hair and yanked her back. He slammed the door and threw her onto the bed in one swift motion. Then he crawled on top of her.

(He's fast.)

Luca crammed his face against hers. His tobacco flavored tongue pried her mouth open and invaded her mouth. Terrified, she chomped down and clenched her jaw. Luca jerked away. Dallas shook her head side-to-side while grinding her teeth. Blood gushed into her mouth. The taste of copper encouraged her. She bit harder and tweaked her head violently. Her teeth pierced until his tongue tore apart. Luca fell back into the booth. Blood sprayed from his mouth, splattering the nudes in the dirty magazines. He whelped in pain and grabbed at his blood-smeared face. Then he laughed.

(An evil, maniacal laugh.)

He tilted his head back and swallowed blood while forcing prolonged eye contact with her. Then Luca smiled with bloody teeth. The whole caboose began to rumble and quake.

"Daw-wes," he whispered her name through his blood spray.

Dallas scrambled out of the filthy bed with his tongue still in her mouth. Chomping and grinding on the hunk of raw flesh, she dashed toward the exit. Luca blocked her. Dallas spat his mangled tongue at him. Then, swaying and keeping her balance in the rumbling train, she ran back to the middle of the car. The caboose rattled and shook worse than it would while racing down tracks.

(Up.)

Dallas climbed the narrow stairs to the cupola above. Once inside the little lookout, she wrestled the sliding window open. Her fixator stuck to the control panel where so many conductors had steered their trains. Luca climbed after her. Having the tactical advantage, Dallas stomped on his head. Three kicks to the face with her steel toes forced him to tumble down. This time, he stayed down. He lost consciousness.

(Breathe. You got this.)

Dallas pounded her fists against her fixator, jerking and yanking frantically until somehow it broke free. She threaded her fixator through the window, then climbed through, but then her hips got stuck. She flutter kicked, wiggled, and squeezed. Finally, she toppled onto the rumbling roof. She stood. She screamed a warrior battle cry into the night, while pumping her fixator in the air victoriously.

"Rrrrawlrrrrr!"

She gasped and panted, overcome by both panic and a wild sense of exultation.

(I fought him off!)

The terror of the attack, the sheer sense of inevitability, it ran together with her almost bloodthirsty elation at hurting him back.

(God. I made the fucker bleed!)

But now.

(Shit. Where? Where to go?)

She heard his unnerving laughter from inside.

(He's awake.)

Dallas ran to the end of the caboose and climbed down the rusty ladder attached to the outside of the car. Once her boots hit the gravel, she sprinted off toward the street, past the Pic-A-Part sign at the entrance, and south on Boulder Highway. She ran and ran. She pumped both her good and bad arms in what would have been a perfect stride if she didn't have to lift her elbow so far away from her body to keep from banging her hardware against her side. After a block, she stopped.

(Will he pursue? Where to go? Home? He lives next door.)

Dallas sprinted again. Her mind screamed. Her lungs burned.

(Move. Move. Run! Don't give him time to catch you.)

Instinctively, she ran toward home. A mile passed. Thoughts raced with her.

(He'll come home sooner or later. What to do then? Tell Maricela? Lock my doors and hope? Can't live like that, not day after day. How the hell to deal with this guy? The police. Go to the police. They'll help. Luca needs to be locked up. God, who knows how often he's done this before. But.)

Dallas looked down at her blood-drenched shirt. Her heart hammered in her chest.

(His blood. It's Luca's blood. What if they blame me? I could end up in jail again.)

Rewind.

[How'd I get here? I'm a strong, educated black woman. An engineer in a hydropower plant. A month ago, I had my life together. I even saved Hoover Dam. So how'd I wind up getting assaulted by my next-door neighbor in a Vegas junkyard? Let's go back to the beginning...]

2

Water Hammer

Her control panel sparkled like the Vegas Strip on a Friday night. Multiple warning indicators screamed about a malfunction on Turbine No. 6. Then the telltale thumping of water bouncing through the massive penstock made the floor rumble. Back pressure threatened to burst the bunker deep inside Hoover Dam. A water hammer behind the hydro-power plant meant imminent disaster.

Last week, Dallas Mack had demonstrated the concept of water hammers for her interns by quickly switching off a full-blast faucet in the break room. She taught them to listen for the knocking pipe that followed. Her impressed trainees pointed and whispered comments as they observed the faucet rattle and bounce with a rapping sound. Repeating that nifty exercise over and over the past decade had ingrained the danger deep into her mind.

So when she heard the first bang, she knew something must have suddenly blocked the eighty-foot channel flowing beneath the cavernous turbine hall. She had to release the back-pressure or the tunnel would blow. The turbine hall would flood in minutes. Hundreds of workers and tourists could drown. Not a swimmer, Dallas didn't like her chances.

(I'll have to crash it.)

Dallas dashed out of the control room and into the main turbine hall. Without time for further internal debate, she jumped onto her four-ton Toyota forklift and turned the key. She punched the plastic cover of the same speed limiter she had installed under the dash a few months ago. A ragged, broken edge sliced into her knuckles. She tore off the entire device and tossed it. Crimson blood oozed from her dark skin, ran down the back of her hand, and dropped into thick dots by her work boots. Ignoring the pain, she yanked a lever and threw the forklift into reverse.

Beep, beep, beep.

The automatic backup alarm echoed through the shaking turbine hall as she slammed the accelerator against the floor. Once far enough away, she stomped the brake with her steel-toes and shifted into drive. The wheels locked, leaving four-foot skid marks on the ground. Tires spun in place until they gripped the concrete floor. She sped through a cloud of burnt rubber and aimed the safety-orange forks directly at Turbine No. 6. As the forklift gained momentum, Dallas fastened her seatbelt over her navy-blue coveralls and prepared to crash. The cavernous bunker rumbled and quaked. She tightened the chinstrap on her yellow hard hat while checking the speedometer. It read 18.8 mph with less than a hundred feet until impact.

"Faster. Go, go, go!"

Dallas steered the forks toward a metal panel on the broad side of Turbine No. 6. The speedometer hit 24.2 as she braced for the collision. She took a deep breath, allowing the smell of motor oil and ozone to comfort her. The forks pierced and penetrated deep into the dead turbine. When the lift slammed into the bulwark, her head snapped forward then back again, like the momentum of a water hammer.

Dallas rolled her shoulders to stretch out the whiplash as she pulled two levers. The forks tilted up and then lifted higher, tearing apart the jammed turbine. Fatigued metal surrendered. Tiny cracks and fractures grew into gaping holes. Broken bits fell as the forks rose overhead. With a broken chunk of the turbine out of the pit and her forks at max height, she stretched under the wreckage to see into the floor.

(Yes!)

Relief slowed her racing heart. She had opened a hole large enough for water to flow again. Then suddenly, the pent up pressure blasted through the remaining blockage in the pit. Within seconds, thousands of gallons of water gushed into the Colorado river below.

(Crisis averted.)

Silvester Schustermann ran onto the scene as fast as his paunchy body could manage. The middle-aged engineering supervisor gave the remaining half of Turbine No. 6 a quick once over. He looked up and gestured one of his pudgy hands at Dallas, directing her to move her load.

"Belgium! You did it," he shouted with a gigantic smile.

"Forty-two, Sil." She saluted her boss and honked her horn twice.

Once her supervisor stepped away from the wreckage, Dallas moved the debris to the side and lowered it. Then she switched off the forklift, hopped out, and met Silver back at Turbine No. 6. He congratulated her with a hug that turned intimate as soon as they touched. Her soft cheek brushed up against his titanium eyeglasses as he looked up at her. Even when trying to pull away, her lips grazed his gray-streaked goatee in a near-miss kiss. Awkwardly, they broke contact and acted paranoid. Dallas stepped back, straightened up, and stood tall, nearly six inches over him. Synchronized, they turned toward the debris hoping nobody noticed their embrace. Side-by-side, they gazed past torn and twisted metal to watch thousands of gallons of Lake Mead water surging beneath them.

"After all these years, the raw power of it still amazes me," Dallas said as she wiped sweat from her brow.

Silver and Dallas roped off the gaping hole in the floor with yellow caution tape. They worked efficiently, like they knew what the other's next move would be before either of them made it. Dallas grabbed a flashlight and climbed down onto a stable perch. She examined pitted metal, cavities, and stress fractures on steel turbine blades.

"Looks like metal fatigue again." She poked at a broken piece.

Silver leaned over the edge, sticking his face into the crater. "It doesn't add up. I triple checked the calculations."

"Something must be making the metal deteriorate faster." Dallas touched the torn housing.

"We'll have to do a post-incident analysis. Climb out of there now. You make me nervous. I can't tell how secure that rig is, Dal."

"It's rock solid." Dallas banged on a hunk of twisted metal with the handle of her foot-long Maglite. A piece tumbled past her feet and got swept away by the geyser gushing under her.

"Enough, Dallas. Take my hand." Silver reached down for her. They clasped wrists. The wounds on her knuckles split open wider, bleeding again. He hoisted her up as her makeshift platform slipped away under her feet. Dangling,

Dallas kicked against the broken turbine. She scrambled up to the floor and landed out of breath.

"Jesus, Dal, you terrify me when you push it like that." Silver pulled her to her feet, and they held onto each others' hands.

"Didn't I save the day?"

"Don't you always?"

"That's why you love me." Dallas batted her eyelashes as a half-joke.

"There are so many reasons."

Breaking the mood, Dallas fingered his simple, gold wedding band. Her flirty smile faded into bitter reality. She broke eye contact with him to scowl at that treacherous piece of jewelry. To emphasize her displeasure, she spun the ring around his finger. He ignored the gesture, so she dropped his hands. Without a word, she retreated to examine the extracted half of Turbine No. 6. She picked up an adjustable wrench and went to work.

Three of her engineering co-workers approached to gawk at Turbine No. 6. Dallas glanced over her shoulder at them. Secretly, she called them the *Three Amigos*. Not because they were Latino, but because they were a trio of gringo idiots. The tallest one looked like a young Chevy Chase and stood nearly eye-to-eye with six-foot-tall Dallas. The one with his hair bleached all-white, his name was Steve. And the little, red-headed guy was a modest mouse named Todd who followed the other two around everywhere. Always, It took all three of them to do a single job. For years and years, Dallas never trusted those guys. She found their incompetence irritating.

(Except Clark. He's funny. And smart.)

"Thanks to Ms. Mack's quick thinking–" Silver gestured toward Dallas.

Bent over and elbow deep in turbine wreckage, she barely heard him over the constant hum. The Three Amigos looked at her and waved. Somehow, they had begun to grow on her. The little one's mouth gaped open. She thought Todd might drool like a fool.

"Mack," Silver called to her. "Mack, come here."

Dallas hustled over to the men. They stood in a semi-circle around her as she re-enacted the incident for them. Steve, the white-haired one, looked bored. And she wished the little ginger would shut his mouth before a bug flew into it. Silver's phone rang, and he stepped aside to take the call. Dallas focused on Clark, the amigos competent leader.

"So, I knew it was a water hammer—"

"We heard it too, Mack. We were working on Turbine No. 14. Doing maintenance. Todd here conked his head real bad," Clark said.

Todd nodded like a dummy, while he touched a lump on his noggin and winced in pain.

"Where's your hard hat?" Dallas pointed at his head.

Todd reached up at his blazing orange hair.

"God dammit, Todd." Dallas shook her head.

Silver flipped his ancient mobile phone shut and returned to the group. "Claims adjusters will be down to inspect this afternoon. Don't touch anything until they finish their report."

"What about our post-incident analysis?" Dallas asked.

"I said. 'Don't touch anything,' Mack."

A desert gecko scurried between her feet and into the center of their cluster. Dallas flinched and grabbed Silver's arm. Without hesitation, he stomped on the lizard, smashing it with his heavy, steel-toed boot.

"Why'd you kill it?" Dallas whispered in his ear.

Annoyed, Silver avoided lifting his foot and shifted his weight off the squishy mess. Steve noticed the way Dallas held Silver's arm, then shot his Amigos a mockingly lustful look.

"Why don't you call it a day, Ms. Mack? We'll start again tomorrow," Silver said.

"You're sending me home?"

"Yes. Go home, Ms. Mack."

(Ouch! What a slap in the face.)

Overlooked and undervalued by dam management, Dallas usually rolled with the punches. But this time, Silver's cold and detached tone cut her to the bone.

Dallas marched away. "Well then, I'll see you tomorrow."

She could not have been more wrong.

3

∩

Silver Flux

Dallas squeezed the two metal prongs of the sparker. *Click click.*

She struck it again, and it spit fiery particles into the gas wake of her oxy-fueled blowtorch. A blue-hot flame ignited and glowed like a tiny lightsaber. Smiling, she lowered the face shield of her welding helmet with her leather gloved hand.

A gift from Silver, a modest boombox on her workbench kept her company. She had programmed her favorite Motown station on every preset button, so that if someone got in her space and messed with her radio, she could get back to where she belonged with her fat, gloved fingers. With less than an hour to go in her shift, Martha and the Vandellas sang about a heat wave. Dallas bopped and bounced along with music inside her bulky welding suit.

She liquified the flux that joined a curved arch to a frame that she spent the whole day assembling. After missing three days of work and spending the long Veteran's Day weekend at home, Dallas couldn't wait to get back to this project. As usual, she worked alone in the mechanics' cage next to the storage area behind Turbine No. 10.

(My fortress of solitude deep inside Hoover Dam.)

"Where's your fire spotter?" Silver asked. He pulled the chain link door shut behind him as he entered her domain. The gate rattled, and he lowered the latch, isolating them behind black slats woven into the fence.

Dallas finished her join, switched off her torch, and lifted her face shield. "You're funny."

"I'm serious, Dal. You know you can't weld in here alone. It's an OSHA violation."

"Really? You send me home 'pending an investigation,' then when I finally get back to work, you bust my balls about this?" Dallas tossed her extinguished torch onto the workbench. She yanked her heavy leather cuffs free and threw her gloves at Silver. He ducked. The thick mitts flew past his head and hit the cage wall. Then they landed on the concrete floor.

Thwack.

"Give me a break, Dal. The guys upstairs are breathing down my neck."

"Right, because it's all about you, Sil."

Silver pushed his slipping bifocals up the bridge of his nose. "You know that's not true."

"Bullshit."

"Dal, be fair."

"Fair? You have some nerve throwing that word around. I'll tell you what's not fair—"

"Please don't—"

"What's not fair is being your top engineer and only getting paid as a junior tech." She beat the side of a busted housing with her ball-peen hammer to punctuate her sentence.

Clang.

"Dal?"

"What's not fair is bumping my negro head against this glass ceiling for the past ten years while watching less experienced *men*, and less intelligent *men*, some *men* that barely speak English, get promoted over me."

Clang, clang.

Diana Ross backed her up with the Supremes on the radio. "Dal."

"What's not fair is being the only woman in this power plant and not having a single, solitary female friend down here."

Clang, clang, clang.

"Dallas, stop!"

"What's not fair is banging my boss for the past six years and having nothing to show for it except facing another holiday season alone." Dallas beat her frustration into the now lumpy and useless piece of aluminum.

Clang, clang, clang, clang, bang.

"You're upset." Silver caressed her flexed wrist, and Dallas relaxed and released the hammer. Silver caught it and held it for her.

"Damn right, I'm upset."

"If it helps, Human Resources said you could use your vacation time for last week so that you won't miss any pay."

"Fuck you, Silver."

"What? Wasn't that supportive?" Silver shrugged and let the hammer rest on the oil stained floor.

Dallas glared at him in disbelief.

(Forcing me to use my vacation time for involuntary leave? Unfuckingbelievable.)

"Every day, you, and all the other socially retarded engineers around here, say inconsiderate shit like that."

(I ignore the others, but I have higher expectations for you.)

Silver stood side-by-side with her at the workbench. He picked up a socket wrench, worked the ratchet a few times, and put it back in the case where it belonged. Tool by tool, he helped organize her area even though she had never asked. While she berated him, Silver kept silent. He felt anxious, like nothing he did would ever be good enough for her. It became overwhelming.

"Set me free, why don't you, babe?" Dallas sang.

Holding the largest Phillips screwdriver toward the magnetic bar mounted to the wall, Silver got angry. Suddenly, the screwdriver shot out of his hand and flew through the air. It slammed into its vacant space on the rack among her other hand tools.

Clang!

"Whoa, what was that?" Dallas asked.

"Metal and magnets do weird things down here," Silver said stepping back. "Because of the turbines."

Dallas held a smaller screwdriver in the palm of her hand a few inches in front of another vacant spot on the same bar. Nothing happened. She moved her hand closer, and still the tool did not move. Touching the shaft to the magnet finally made it stick.

"Really?" She gave him a suspicious look.

"Why do you always have to challenge me?"

"Isn't that what makes me so attractive?" Dallas danced and sang along with the Motown chorus. "You just keep me hanging on."

"If a guy said and did these things, Dal. It would be—"

"Gay."

"I was going to say insubordination, Dal."

"You treat me like shit whenever someone's watching."

"I'm a professional."

"And I'm not?"

"I didn't say that. But, sometimes you behave inappropriately."

"Wow. Now I'm inappropriate," Dallas said, getting angry.

"There's a time and place."

"I'm not having this conversation again, Sil. I'm not ashamed of us."

"That's because you have nothing to lose."

"And fuck you. Again." Her face grew red-hot with anger. Her heart rate rose. Her breathing quickened. Her muscles tensed. At the same time, Silver blushed. Beads of perspiration formed on his graying brow. His chest heaved behind his significant beer belly. Diana Ross faded into the Dazz Band plucking an electric guitar and singing about whipping it. Silver focused on a yard of cut, heavy chain on the work bench in front of him, and it fell to the floor.

Rattle, cling, cling, tink.

Dallas locked eyes with Silver. He tore off her welding hood with one hand and grabbed a fistful of her flat ironed, shoulder length, black hair with the other. Her head yielded, exposing the lean muscular lines of her neck. Silver buried his face in her favorite spot under her ear. He licked, bit, and sucked all at once. Dizzy from him, Dallas nearly collapsed. Silver shoved her against a curtain of heavy chain hanging from pegs on the block wall behind her. Groping through, the links clung to her, and somehow, her knees had enough strength to stand.

Silver bound Dallas by wrapping chains around both her wrists and hooking them to pegs overhead. Dressed in her welding gear, Dallas hung helplessly. He'd never seen anything sexier in his life. Her mahogany eyes gazed into his ice blue ones. They were the same, yet opposite, and they could not resist each other.

He tore down her overalls' zipper in one quick swish and yanked open her shirt snaps, exposing her red lace bra. Her breasts heaved with each and every touch. At this moment, she felt like they were the only two people in the whole dam. Silver, however, remained acutely aware that anyone could walk into the cage at any moment.

With the speed of a man racing against the clock, Silver unbuckled his belt and unzipped his pants. Dallas wanted to stroke the raging erection that struggled to break free from his boxer shorts, but her hands were completely bound over her head. She tested the chains and honestly could not break free.

(How did he tie me up so fast?)

Bill Withers sang about being used, and Dallas swayed her hips with the groovy funk of the base and percussion. Silver unbuttoned her jeans and tugged them down over her plump ass and wide hips. He groped at her matching red thong until it fell to her ankles. Kissing her firm, flat tummy, he untied her left boot and set her leg free. She kicked off the Timberland, and her wool sock dangled half on and half off. Silver palmed the back of her left knee and lifted her leg out of her clothes. Forcing her hips open, he pulled her thigh high above her waist. He bit and sucked on the inside of her leg, then wrapped a dangling chain around her thigh twice. He secured a link to another peg above her.

With Dallas at his mercy and hanging half-spread-eagle, Silver released his average-sized cock from its polyester-blend prison. In one thrust, he entered her deeply. She gasped and pulled on her chains to clutch his pasty-white ass with her suspended, muscular calf. As quickly as he started fucking her, he finished.

Leaving her hanging, he withdrew and repackaged himself in record time. As he tucked in his shirt and got presentable, she tugged on the chains.

"Uh, this feels a little confining."

"Oh, right," Silver said. He slipped the links off their hooks, and her arms and leg surrendered to gravity.

"Do you know where your towel is?" Dallas asked, gesturing toward his messy jizz running down her leg.

"That's a good one," Silver laughed at the reference to *The Hitchhiker's Guide to the Galaxy*.

"Ugh, thanks. But you know, Adams had a point." Dallas fumbled out of the wrist chains and grabbed an oily rag off the ground. Still balancing on one foot, she wiped the evidence of their sex act off her unbound thigh. She threw the rag to the floor and untwisted the chain from around her leg. Link marks ached as her quad relaxed. She massaged the dents out of her thigh while stepping back into her jeans and her coveralls. By the time she had zipped up, she discovered Silver had made it halfway to the cage exit.

"Can we finish this later tonight?" Dallas asked.

Silver peeked out the gate, and once he felt assured the coast was clear, he closed it again. "I can't tonight, the boys have a soccer game after school." He checked his watch. "Actually, I have to get going, or I'll miss the whole first half."

"Of course." She looked hurt as she rubbed the link marks that were already forming bruises on her wrists. With one sloppy-socked foot, she followed him to the exit, carrying her boot by the laces.

Silver tucked her mussed hair behind her ear. "How about I swing by your place after? I'll bring Vietnamese take out. Archie's? Your favorite."

"I'd love that."

"It's a date." He looked at his watch again. "How about seven-ish?"

"I'll be waiting."

"You're my forty-two," Silver said. He gave her a peck on the cheek and dashed away.

Dallas stepped into her boot and bent over to tie it. "He'll take care of me later," she said, trying to reassure herself. But she was wrong again, and as much as she didn't want to admit it to herself, she knew he wouldn't follow through. "Fine. I have someone waiting for me at home too."

4

Scrabble Squabble

"*A-F-F-A-I-R*. Affair. That's one, plus three, plus three, plus one, and one, and one equals ten; all on the triple word score, so thirty points for me," Maricela said as she scribbled her score into her new leather-bound *Scrabble* notebook.

"I bought you that so that you could journal," Dallas said while tapping Maricela's mahogany dining room table.

"This is how I journal," Maricela snarked through a congested haze of tobacco smoke.

"Journaling is about your feelings." Dallas reached behind her and flicked on the antique ceiling fan.

"Nothing makes me feel better than a good game of *Scrabble*," Maricela said.

"I think you missed my point." Dallas sat back and patted her lap. Her hairless Chinese Crested terrier jumped up and licked her face.

"Have I?"

Disinterested in the verbal dodge-and-parry, Dallas turned her focus toward her dog. "Who's my baby? Who's my Bella?" she asked as she cradled her pet in her arms and nuzzled the dog's smooth neck.

"Maybe one day, you'll graduate to an actual, human baby."

Dallas rolled her eyes.

(Blunt and abrasive. What's new? We probably would never have become friends if we weren't neighbors. Seven years living next to this woman, and now we're like sisters. We certainly fight like sisters.)

Maricela loved Dallas more than her own twin, who, despite living in North Las Vegas, had not visited in the past decade. And Dallas? Dallas had not seen any of her family in five years.

"I'm ahead by over a hundred points. You all better step up." Maricela turned to her seventeen-year-old son, Ramone, sitting on her right. "Your turn, honey."

"Lame," Ramone said as he pouted and crossed his arms. He dropped his chin and hid behind his long raspberry-slushy-blue bangs. "Can't we play something cool, like Xbox?"

"Now honey, you know Tuesdays are family night."

"I can find a group game for us on Xbox, Mom."

"No. We do board games in the dining room like a real family on Tuesday nights."

"Could we at least play something cool, like *Cards Against Humanity*?" Ramone asked.

"You know I don't approve of that game. And *Scrabble* helps Luca with his English." Maricela smiled at her obscenely younger husband sitting on her left.

"Pft," Luca said as he exhaled pipe smoke over the game-board, adding more haze to the already choked room.

Even though Dallas hated second-hand smoke, Luca's tobacco smelled like a musky, sweet cherry. She found it oddly comforting. Smoke lingered over the table, infusing with the smell of Maricela's Mexican cooking. Dallas finger-combed Bella's long hair out of her eyes. Her dog's two-toned face had long white hair on one side. The other side looked like a large furry black eye-patch. Dallas parted Bella's hair and tied pretty pink bows on each side to make pigtails.

"Hey Dal, we oughta dye Bella's hair blue," Ramone said. "Her white parts would take Manic Panic perfectly."

Dallas held her dog up in the air like an inspecting kennel club judge. Mottled pink and black patches and dots covered the dog's bald body. Fur wisps punctuated Bella's crest, plume, and socks. The dog had a black tail and eye-patch, but the rest of her fur was pure white.

"We could do it in my bath tub," Ramone offered.

"What a mess. No way. I'm not cleaning that up," Maricela objected.

"Seriously, she'd look awesome." He ignored his mother.

"Ramone, you're holding up the game." Maricela tapped her pencil against her *Scrabble* book impatiently. A second generation Mexican-American, Maricela had worked as a social worker her whole life. Normally on these nights, she talked about how she wanted to spend her time after retirement. She only had eight years to go before she could finally call it quits.

Ramone slid the letter *T* onto the board, spelling the word *A-T*.

"Really? You can do better," Maricela scolded her son.

"I don't want to do better."

"Fine, only two points for Ramone then."

"My turn," Dallas said. She spelled out the word *T-O-R-Q-U-E* on the mostly ignored quadrant of the board. "That's triple on the Q."

"Impressive." Maricela slid the tiles and verified the bonus claim. Then she added her friend's score. "You could catch me. Glad your head's in the game and not on that *tramposo.*"

"Who's a cheater?" Ramone asked.

"Why do you have to do that?" Dallas asked.

"Do what?" Maricela replied.

"Jab at me about him every chance you get." Dallas shifted Bella in her lap.

"I don't know what you're talking about."

Dallas pointed at the board, "Infidelity. Cheap. Lonely. Affair. I sense a theme here."

"Infidelity was a seventy-three point word." Maricela referred to her scorebook. "I also played. Help. Scared. Abuse. But you don't think that means anything, do you?"

"I love him, you know." Dallas hugged her dog.

"You're not listening, Dallas. Not everything is about you." Maricela's eyes darted back and forth from the board to Luca.

"What?" Dallas asked.

"I also played... Help. Scared. Mistreated. Abuse." She gave a sideways glance at her husband again.

"Christ's sake, Mom." Ramone glared at Dallas. "*Nos bate.*"

(What?)

"*Que sólo se casó con una tarjeta verde,*" Ramone mumbled without looking up from his phone.

Luca blew smoke at the teenager and said nothing.

"Shut up, Ramone," Maricela said. She spelled out her next word on her rack. "Nice try, but I'm not sending you to your room. That's where the Xbox is."

"I'm telling you, green card marriage," Ramone repeated his point to Dallas.

"En Espanõl, or he'll understand you," Maricela warned her son.

"Mierda! Watch this. I'll use big words and say them fast. And *número dos* here won't have a clue what I'm talking about," Ramone said to his mother. Then the teenager smiled respectfully and looked at his step-father. "Is that not accurate? You paranoid, glittery, *Twilight* fart? You surmise that I'm articulating compliments about you. But you harbor a manic, aggressive temper and a penchant for corporal punishment, you matriarch fornicator." Ramone smiled with pride at his mother.

"Where's that impressive vocabulary in the game? I don't see it here." Maricela waved the *Scrabble* book in Ramone's face then turned to her husband. "Luca, it's your turn."

Handsome enough to be a Calvin Klein model, Thirty-something Luca sucked his pipe. He had emigrated from somewhere in Romania during the Bosnian war. Dallas didn't know exactly where Luca came from, but he had a stern, Eastern European look. He talked slowly and with a thick accent that reminded her of Bela Lugosi in that black-and-white *Dracula* film. Dallas had always admired Luca's striking features.

(I see exactly why she fell for him.)

Luca slid his letter tiles behind his wooden tile holder, using it as the privacy barrier. After a significant game delay, he spelled the word *F-R-I-G-A-R-E* downward, using the *F* that Maricela placed on her turn.

"Two *G* points," Luca said.

Maricela frowned, then she softened. "That's not English, Luca." She removed the tiles from the game board and scooted over to help him. Luca stiffened and looked embarrassed. The couple pushed letters back and forth and talked for almost minute.

"*Curva!*" Luca stomped his fist on the table so hard that everyone's tiles fell off their stands.

No one knew that word meant whore. But Ramone and Dallas could tell that the degrading curse was directed toward Maricela. She took a deep breath and composed herself, then calmly placed three of Luca's wooden tiles on the board and spelled *R-A-G-E* for him.

"See, double word score. Rage. That means anger." Maricela stood and addressed the room, "If you'll excuse me." She disappeared into the downstairs bathroom.

"I know what means," Luca said shouting after her. His tobacco-stained teeth bit on the smooth stem of his one-of-a-kind pipe as he sucked more smoke.

Against her better judgment, Dallas fell captive to the hand-carved, ebony piece. The twists and curves of the bowl manifested as a different beast every time she gazed at it. Talons stretched toward the pipestem dangling from his tight lips. Then as Luca turned his head, the pipe's bowl looked more like a toothy sea-monster. Transfixed on the surreal creature, Dallas felt both frightened and intrigued. Luca looked down at his new *Scrabble* letters and the teeth of his pipe morphed into living bark and thorns. He caught her staring.

"What?" Luca exhaled smoke from his nostrils.

"Your pipe," Dallas said. "It's remarkable."

Luca released the sculpture from his mouth and held it in front of her face so that she could appreciate its silhouette. Dallas reached out to touch the gnarly knuckles of what now looked like a claw.

Luca jerked the pipe away from her. "No touch."

"Sorry," Dallas said, placing her palm on the table like a scolded child.

"I bring from Romania. From my family, Dracul." Luca tapped the spent tobacco remains into a crystal ashtray and set the pipe on a matching hand-carved stand.

"Ugh, not this Dracula *mierda* again," Ramone said without looking up from his phone.

"You respect! Vlad great man."

"Whatever, dude. If Romania is so great," Ramone said as his phone glitched and froze, "Why did you come to this racist shithole of America?"

"Silence!" Luca pounded both fists on the table.

Letter tiles bounced, a few flipped over. Bella barked at Luca and then growled. Dallas wrapped her arms around her dog and rearranged her tiles on their stand.

"Vlad can suck this," Ramone gestured to his cock.

Luca grabbed the board with both hands and hurled it at Ramone's head. The teen ducked in time to avoid getting hit. The game-board smashed into a monumental five-foot nickel-plated crucifix hanging on the wall behind him. An emaciated metallic Jesus swayed on his massive cross as tiles scattered in a shot-blast pattern and bounced on the hardwood floor. Bella barked and lunged for Luca. Dallas yanked her dog's pink collar back in time to avoid Luca's backhanded fist. The two little heart-shaped pink tags on Bella's zirconia-crusted collar swung upward and hovered parallel to the floor. Dallas tapped the metal hearts, and they rebounded, pointing toward Luca.

"Enough!" Luca clenched his teeth so tight that they ground.

Scretch, crunch, crunch.

Dallas winced at the sound. Quickly, she stowed her terrier in her messenger bag. She backed her chair away from the table and crept toward the door. Having heard the game board crash, a red-eyed Maricela reappeared from the bathroom.

(*I should help them.*)

"I'm gonna go." Dallas walked backward into the foyer. No one heard her or noticed her retreat. Keeping her eyes fixed on the dining room, she felt for the doorknob behind her. Once she touched it, she gave it a twist and slid through the door to escape. As soon as Dallas stepped outside, Bella jumped out of the bag and darted into the night. Dallas slammed the front door and ran down the street after her dog. She lost sight of Bella immediately.

"Bella! Bella come back," Dallas cried out into the darkness.

(*Now I'm truly alone.*)

5

Baby Bella

Dallas screamed. Her blood-chilling shriek echoed off the pastel stucco houses and through the suburban streets of her sleepy Henderson neighborhood. Her bag slipped off her shoulder, sending a hundred freshly-printed pink *Missing Dog* flyers cascading across her front porch. A fierce gust tumbled the papers over landscape rock in her front yard. Several flyers wrapped around the handles of the erected hedge shears. Viscous, drying blood smeared onto the pastel paper.

"Bella!" Dallas dove across her postage stamp front yard. Sharp rocks jabbed her kneecaps as she collapsed next to her dog. Pain shot up her thigh, and she wailed again. "No. No, no, no! Bella?"

The gruesome scene of Bella's death instantly burned an afterimage into her brain. Dallas closed her eyes to stop the horror from being associated with this visual memory, but it was too late. With her eyes shut, she saw the garden shearer handles rammed six inches into the ground like a horrific, A-frame armature. The twelve-inch blade of her hedge shears pierced her dog's rectum. The double-blade emerged through the dog's abdominal cavity and neck.

Bella's head tilted to the side, and the blade tips protruded from a raspberry-slushy-blue tuft of hair over her left ear. The dog's drying blood stained the pink ponytail bow.

"Why are you blue?" Dallas whispered as she opened her eyes. Her question delivered a sick gut punch that made her want to scream, cry, and vomit all at once. She did none of those things. Instead, she froze. Paralyzed.

Ramone's voice echoed in her head, "Hey Dal, we oughta die her hair blue."

(No. No. Ramone didn't do this. He couldn't.)

She tried to suppress the *Scrabble* memory. But it jabbed at her mind like a splinter under a fingernail. Dallas wanted to cuddle her fur baby, to ease Bella's pain and make it all better, but the graphic gore killed any impulse to touch her dog. Repulsed. The most brutal part of the butchering finally clicked in her mind. Someone—

(Was it Ramone?)

Someone had slit Bella from chest to belly and pulled out her heart, lungs, liver, and intestines. The organs cascaded from Bella's abdomen in a gruesome display. Some warning. A threat.

(But why? Why would Ramone dye her blue, and—)

Nasty, green-backed flies buzzed around the carcass. A trail of red fire ants ate from the puddle of blood. Bella's tail soaked in it. Dallas looked at the tapered, flat-top of her hedgerow, and blamed herself for leaving her garden tools in the yard. She cried, wanting to nuzzle her baby girl for comfort, and then sobbed harder knowing that she'd never be able to do that again.

(I can't touch her. I just can't.)

Dallas had an aversion to dead things.

(Necrophobia, someone called it once.)

For as long as she could remember, she could never touch anything dead. Not a person. Not an animal. Not even an insect. Nothing. Not even her dead puppy. Her precious baby Bella.

Dallas crawled back to her crumpled bag on the concrete. She fumbled through her things, forcing herself to look away from her dead dog. Once she found her iPhone, she dialed 9-1-1.

A dispatcher answered, "Nine-one-one, what is your emergency?"

"Someone killed my dog," Dallas sobbed.

"What's the address?"

"Seven-sixty-five Palo Verde Lane, Henderson."

"What is your name?"

"Dallas Mack."

"Ms. Mack, are you in danger?"

(I don't know.)

The killer might still be—out there. Hyper-vigilant, Dallas stood and surveyed the deserted street. It seemed quiet. Maybe no one heard her scream. Most likely, her neighbors heard and chose to ignore her cry for help—the Vegas way. She fixated on Maricela's house, looking for signs of Ramone.

(He could be watching me from inside.)

"Ma'am? Are you still there?"

"Yes, I'm here."

"Are you in danger?"

Dallas scooped up her bag, backed up the steps, and dashed into her house. She secured the lock behind her. "I—I don't know. I'm back inside now. I locked the door."

"Good."

"My dog's outside. She's—it's horrible," Dallas cried.

"Two units are on their way. They should be there in a few minutes."

"I was going to work, and I walked outside and found my dog. She's all cut up. Someone stabbed her. Her guts are everywhere. He impaled her with one of my garden tools." Dallas peeked out her front window. Bella's dead eyes stared back at her. Dallas broke out in sobs again.

"Are you alone in the house?"

"Yes."

"Are all the doors and windows locked?"

"Yes."

"Can you give me your physical description?"

"Sure. I'm six-feet tall, dark-skinned African-American, female…"

"What are you wearing today?"

"I'm wearing jeans and a blue button-down shirt. I'm on my way to work. Oh shit, I have to call work." Dallas checked the time on her phone. She was already running late before all this started.

A siren chirped around the corner, red and blue lights flashed through the cracks in the blinds.

"They're here. Thank you," Dallas said as she hung up and texted Silver. "911 at home. Police here. Will be late."

Dallas dashed out the front door as the Las Vegas Metro squad car pulled into her cul-de-sac and parked under the olive tree in front of her house. In a panic, Dallas charged toward the passenger side of the cruiser. Two police officers stepped out from opposite sides of the car at the same time. She found herself looking down at a short cop who looked like an ex-Marine. He gestured *stop* with a stiff arm, warning her to keep her distance. She froze in her tracks and took three steps back.

"Officer..." She squinted to read his name tag from a distance. "Garrison. My dog. My Bella's dead. She's right there." Dallas pointed over the hedges.

The driving officer proceeded around the car with his hand on his pistol. He surveyed the scene, looking for threats. "Please step back, ma'am."

Dallas backpedaled past her parked Subaru Forester and up her short driveway. She made no sudden moves and kept her hands halfway in the air. Both officers had buzz cuts and wore dark sunglasses, making them seem more robotic than human. On this chilly Vegas morning, they wore long sleeve khaki shirts with bullet proof vests underneath. They advanced up her narrow driveway and squeezed between her slate-blue SUV and the hedges until they caught their first glimpse of the dog. Dallas noticed a slight flinch on Garrison's face, but otherwise, they held their emotionless expressions when confronted by the gore.

The officers approached the skewered dog with a mechanical demeanor. Garrison put on blue nitrile gloves and moved a couple of rocks near one of the tool handles. Then he pointed at the tip of the blade sticking out of the dog's skull. "No scratching or dinging on the tip. How'd he hammer the handles into the ground?"

The big cop shrugged his shoulders.

Dallas walked closer. She caught a glimpse of the big cop's name tag.

(McCoy.)

"Stand back, ma'am," McCoy ordered. "Any sign of forced entry?"

"What? Uh, no," Dallas said, stepping back. "Bella got out the other night, Officer McCoy—"

"You let your dog run loose?" Garrison asked.

"No, never. Well, not normally. She was upset and ran away–"

"You dye your dog blue?" McCoy asked.

"No. I don't."

"It's blue." McCoy pointed.

"She wasn't blue the last time I saw her."

"It's sure blue now," McCoy insisted.

"She's also inside-out, but you'd rather discuss the color of her fur?"

Garrison tore off his gloves and pulled out his mobile phone. He snapped a single photo of Bella, then put his phone away. "Anyone you know, ex-husband, baby-daddy, boyfriend, who might have done this?"

"No. Nobody."

Both cops stared at her from behind their mirrored lenses. The awkward silence lasted an eternity.

"Well. Maybe someone."

The cops gave each other an *I-knew-it* glance.

Dallas hesitated. "My neighbor's son, Ramone." She pointed at Marcela's house next door. "He wanted to dye her fur blue. He walks." She paused to swallow. "He walked, my dog sometimes."

The cops looked at each other. Their faces remained expressionless. Neither of them took notes.

"Ramon Nunez Rosales. He lives right there." Dallas stepped forward and pointed at Maricela's house again.

"Step back ma'am," McCoy warned, his voice loud and stern.

"Aren't you going to do anything?"

"Like what?" Garrison asked.

"Like take my statement. Or interview witnesses. What about evidence? Like forensics?"

"Someone watches too much TV," McCoy said with a mocking smile. "It's a dog. This is Las Vegas. Metro already has a massive backlog of actual people homicides."

(Motherfuckers.)

"So you're not going to do anything?"

"Look ma'am—" McCoy began.

(Do your damn job.)

"It's a threat! It's a bloody mess. You have to do something."

"Has someone made a threat against you?" McCoy asked.

"No. Not directly, but this…" Dallas pointed at her dog. "This sure feels like a threat."

McCoy bent over Bella and put his hands under her forelegs. Then he lifted and slid the stiff dog off the garden blade. Purposely disrespectful, he dropped Bella's sticky body on the rocks.

Thwap.

McCoy yanked the shears out of the ground, and the blood-soaked mud under the rocks made a sucking sound.

Thwup.

The two officers walked behind the squad car. Garrison popped the trunk and pulled out a plastic evidence bin. McCoy dropped the bloody garden tool inside as Garrison got into the car.

"Wait. That's it?" Dallas asked.

"That's it," McCoy said, tearing off his gloves and throwing them in the trunk.

"How do I reach you?"

"Just call Metro," McCoy said. He slammed the trunk shut, reached into his pocket, and handed her a generic business card for the main desk operator.

(Damn cops.)

Dallas gave the card a polite glance. She shook her head. The cops drove away without another word. Dallas stood, completely defeated. She gazed down at the mass of bloody skin and fur that used to be her closest friend in the world. The police had tossed Bella aside like garbage.

(They have no intention of doing anything. They won't help.)

Loneliness overwhelmed her. Helplessness terrified her.

She pulled her phone out of her back pocket. Silver had not texted her back, so she rattled off a new text to him. "Someone killed Bella." She paced back and forth on her porch. No response. She tapped her phone again, "Someone murdered my dog! Cops did nothing!" More pacing. More waiting. Another text, "I NEED YOU!!!" Dallas went inside and slammed the door. She called Silver's cell. It rang once. He answered.

"Hello?" Silver said.

"What the hell?"

"I'm sorry, I think you have the wrong number."

"Oh no, you don't. I don't care if your wife's there. I'm having a crisis here!"

"Nope, that's the wrong number." He hung up on her.

"Fucker!" Furious, Dallas threw her phone down the hall. She growled and screamed and stomped in frustration. Her blood pressure shot through the roof. Then a crash from the kitchen made her nearly jump out of her skin. She tiptoed around the corner to investigate.

"Hello? Who's there?"

Weaponless, she spin-jumped into the doorway and held up her fists like a karate cartoon. No one there. A container of cooking utensils and her block of knives had fallen to the floor. Spatulas, ladels, whisks, serving spoons, and all kinds of knives sprawled across the floor. But not randomly. They all lined up in a row. The blades and business ends of the tools all pointed toward her.

Her phone rang in the living room. Her mood instantly switched. Dallas hopped over the kitchen mess and ran to find her phone. "It's about time," she said. She found it and answered, but Silver was not calling.

Disappointed, she answered, "Hi, Maricela."

"Dal, what the heck's going on over there? I heard screams and saw cops. Are you all right?"

"No. I am not all right." Dallas broke down and cried.

(I need my friend. But she's his mother.)

"I'm coming over," Maricela said.

"Watch out for—" The call dropped. Dallas raced to her front door and yanked it open in time to hear Maricela scream bloody-murder. Maricela ran inside. Out of breath, her heart pounding out of her chest, Maricela slammed the door shut. She pushed her back against it to keep out the evil.

"Sweet baby Jesus—" Maricela crossed herself like a good Catholic. "—Mary, and Joseph. What was that?"

"Bella."

Maricela hugged her friend. Neither one of them wanted to let go.

"What happened?"

"You know how she ran away a few nights ago? Well, I found her this morning."

"Coyotes?" Maricela pulled away from the hug.

"No. Worse. She was. Impaled and mounted on my hedge clippers."

"What? Impaled? Evil, *mal, mal.*" Maricela rubbed the gold St. Michael pendant hanging from her neck.

"What should I do?" Dallas asked. "I already called the cops."

"And?"

Dallas gave her a *you-know-how-it-is* look. "They did nothing. Then I called Silver."

"And he blew you off? Oh honey, I'm so sorry." Maricela hugged her again. "You know what?"

"What?"

"Let's not make this about him. Let's take care of you."

Dallas nodded.

"Let's bury your dog."

Maricela gathered up Bella's favorite doggie blanket from the sofa, and the two friends walked to the front yard together. Dallas picked up a pair of gardening gloves under the hedges, as Maricela laid Bella's blanket on the ground next to the eviscerated terrier.

"Uh. Why is her hair blue, Dal?"

(Don't make me say it.)

Dallas looked at her friend, pleading with her eyes. Then Maricela remembered the doggy hair-dying conversation during *Scrabble* night.

"No way," Marcela said. "Ramones a good kid. *El es bueno.*"

Dallas had no words. Instead of debating her Ramone theory, she contemplated her dog. After carrying Bella around for five years, Dallas knew exactly how much her dog weighed and how to handle her. But she couldn't touch her now.

(Necrophobia.)

"I can't." Dallas handed the leather gloves to Maricela.

"I don't think I can either, Dal"

"I have a thing."

"A thing?"

"I'm necrophobic."

Maricela looked at Dallas with disbelief and empathy with a hint of annoyance. Then she took the gloves and slid them on. When Maricela lifted the gory mess, the dog's hollow body sagged between her hands like a rack of raw pork ribs. The feeling nauseated her as she laid Bella to rest on the pink blanket.

Dallas puked in the sticky blood puddle as green flies buzzed and bit at her neck. Maricela gathered Bella's organs and laid them on the blanket with the rest of the carcass. When Dallas turned away to fetch the garden hose, Maricela carried the dead bundle to the backyard. Gathering herself, Dallas stayed in the front and sprayed away Bella's blood with the hose. A foamy, pink river washed away tiny dried acacia leaves and flowed into the street and down into the gutter.

Dallas cleared landscaping rocks from a spot under another olive tree in her backyard. The calcified dirt refused to surrender to her shovel. Maricela ran across the property line to retrieve her pick-axe from her garden shed. It took them over an hour to break ground. Another hour of hard labor gave them a shallow grave the size of a Timberland shoebox. Dallas cried as Maricela lowered Bella's wrapped body into the hole. Marcela handed her the shovel. Dallas sobbed harder and harder with each shovelful of earth dropped in the grave. At ten o'clock, they finished. Covered in dirt, blood, and tears, Dallas needed a shower.

(I reek.)

"My baby Bella," Dallas whispered. Her phone chimed. It was a text.

Maricela could tell the message came from Silver. "He's got some timing. *Cómo práctico,*"

"I gotta get to work." Dallas sniffled while reading his message.

"Why don't you call off and get some rest? I can stay with you all day," Maricela said in an odd tone that triggered paranoia.

(Wait. What?)

Dallas looked at the fresh grave, and a sinking feeling made her suddenly question her friend's intentions. Maybe Ramone didn't kill Bella.

(Could it have been you?)

"No. I need to get out of here," Dallas said.

"I'll put this stuff away so that you can take a shower."

"No thanks. I'm going to go." Dallas marched toward the front of the house and toward her car. She could not escape Maricela fast enough.

"At least freshen up a bit." Marcela followed after her.

"No time," Dallas said as she jumped behind the wheel of her Subaru.

"Call me later," Maricela yelled through the tinted window.

With her heart racing, Dallas nodded, then backed out of her driveway. She sped away.

6

Verbal Warning

Dallas grabbed her favorite four-pound blacksmith hammer by its solid metal handle. The weathered tool had been forged by her father long ago. Closing her eyes, she recalled one of her favorite memories. It rolled through her mind like a home movie. She saw herself as a child, standing by her Daddy's side as he fashioned the hammer in his busy, but organized garage workshop. At eleven years old, she already stood as tall as him.

(I loved to watch Daddy work.)

Focused. He had such intent. When her father presented her with the tool, he said, "This is yours."

When she felt the incredible weight of this unique hammer for the first time, Dallas gasped. Her hand gripped it naturally. It felt perfectly balanced.

Then her father said, "Every tool is a weapon if you hold it right. But for now, let's build."

(I fell in love with welding that day.)

"You were supposed to come talk to me," Silver shouted over the turbine noise in the bunker, snapping her back to the present.

"I did, but your door was closed," Dallas smirked. "I know what that means."

"I'm a supervisor. I have lots of meetings," he yelled while standing very close to her.

"I know. I know. You're the boss." Dallas saluted him with her father's blacksmith hammer, then started chipping away the busted rod again.

"You should have tried back."

"I figured you'd come find me when you had the time. Isn't that how it always goes?"

"Right." He didn't appreciate her snarky attitude today. "I need you to sign this." Silver handed her a clipboard with a document printed on official Hoover Dam letterhead. *Verbal Warning* screamed at her in big red capital letters across the top.

"Warning? For what?"

"Read it." He pointed at the document.

Dallas skimmed the legalese. "You're writing me up for being late today?"

"You didn't call—"

"The hell I didn't!"

"You need to let me finish speaking, Dallas. I was going to say; you didn't call two hours before the start of your shift. That's the policy."

"My dog died, Silvester! I wasn't going to come to work at all today, but I needed to finish installing this before the weekend." She pointed at a motor inside an open wooden crate. "I'm going home in fifteen minutes, and I'm still not done."

"Well, maybe if you'd been on time."

"Did you *not* hear me? I found Bella murdered this morning!"

"It's just a verbal warning, Dallas."

"Then why is it printed on paper?" She held it in his face. "In color?"

"To document our discussion for your personnel file."

Dallas tore the paper from the clipboard, ripped it in half, and let it flutter to the floor. "Document this." She shoved the clipboard into his chest.

Tired of the yelling match, Silver looked around to be sure no one could hear. "Why don't you come to my office?"

Dallas mocked and mimicked his head movements, "Why? Are you afraid someone will see you being a dick to me? Whatever you have to say, say it to me here. Say it now."

"It's time." Silver stomped his foot. "This needs to end."

"You're firing me?"

"No. I'm breaking up with you, Dallas."

"What? Why?"

Silver pulled her away from the turbine and gestured for her to removed her earplugs. "Look, we can't keep going on like this, Dallas. I'm a married man. And I'm your boss."

"I'm fully aware of both those points. Believe me."

(He's using this morning as an excuse to dump me. Coward.)

"Either we stop working together, or we stop seeing each other. And I'm not going to leave my job here, Dallas."

(Quit repeating my name. Stop trying to manipulate me.)

"Me either, Silvester Schustermann."

Silver stared at her. Then he found the words, "Come on, Dal. Are you really happy?"

(Right now, I'm fucking furious.)

"I needed you this morning. And you weren't there for me. You're never there for me. My poor, poor Bella." Dallas choked back tears, refusing to let him see her cry.

(He doesn't care.)

"You always choose your family over me. You didn't return my texts. I stood over my butchered dog, with cops being... Prick cops. And you wouldn't even talk to me on the phone because Isabel might have heard."

"I wasn't at home. I wasn't with Isabel. I was here at work."

"Oh." She felt like an ass.

"I came in early to prepare a presentation for the Director of Operations," Silver said. "I was in the middle of giving that presentation when you started texting me."

"Oh." She felt even worse.

"It's like you can't take 'no' for an answer, Dal. Hell, you can't even take 'wait a minute' for an answer."

(Wait. How'd he do that? He broke up with me. And yet I feel sorry for him.)

"I'm always waiting for you, but when you want me, I jump like your eager pup–"

(Do not mention the dog again. He just does NOT care.)

"See this isn't working for you either."

"Our connection, Sil. It's so strong. I feel drawn to you. I have since the first time we met. It's irresistible."

"I know, Dal. I feel it too. But there's more to making a relationship work than–"

"Sex?"

"I was going to say animal magnetism, but yes," Silver leaned in to whisper the next word, "Sex." He backed away and spoke at a normal volume again. "Look, if the higher ups find out, we could both lose our jobs. We've been lucky not to be discovered all these years. Why keep pushing it?"

"My job is all I have left."

(I don't want to lose him.)

She paused to listen to her true feelings.

(I never had him. I've just been borrowing him, on and off, for the past six years or so.)

"So we're over?" she asked.

"Yes. It's over."

"Well, that's that."

"Going forward, let's try to keep things professional," Silver said.

"Going forward," she mumbled.

"Alright. Good talk. Have a nice weekend." He hustled away from her to avoid any more awkwardness.

(This is how it will be now.)

She watched him leave, and the further away he got, the more she noticed the waddle in his walk.

(Why have I never noticed that before?)

Considering her unfinished mess of a motor installation all around her, she sighed. Her motivation to work had evaporated.

(I want to go home.)

Then she remembered that Bella wasn't waiting for her anymore, and she didn't want to go to her empty house either. The thought of facing Maricela, Ramone, or Luca gave her the creeps.

(I have no one and nowhere.)

She pulled a red-and-white striped laminated caution tag out of her coverall pocket and scribbled her initials on the engineer's line with a Sharpie. Then she attached the lock-out tag to her project with a zip-tie.

(No one touches this except me.)

"Tough shit. This'll have to wait until Monday. I'm out of here." As she abandoned her project, her pace quickened. By the time she walked halfway to her locker, she found herself jogging. Like Superman, she unzipped her coveralls while running full speed. After she had reached her locker, she stepped out of her navy-blue jumpsuit and threw it into the laundry bin. Like an expert safecracker, she spun the dial on her padlock, yanked it open and retrieved her bag. In a hurry to go nowhere, in particular, she raced to the time clock, punched out, and dashed into the elevator.

"Faster. Faster," she muttered impatiently, tapping her foot as the lift carried her up. Like a claustrophobic miner escaping the depths of Hell, Dallas gasped for air. When the doors parted, she raced to safety and comfort of her parked car.

Finally alone on the drive home, Dallas felt herself relax. Somewhere between Boulder City and Henderson, she relaxed too much and dozed off behind the wheel. A yellow Porsche Boxster cut her off on its way to the exit ramp. When Dallas woke, brake lights collided with her front bumper. She stomped her brake and jerked the steering wheel toward the shoulder. The Subaru careened toward a sound barrier, hit the guardrail and bounced like a pinball back into the exit lane. She spun and skidded past the end of the wall. Overcompensating, Dallas made the wrong move, and the blue Subaru flipped over a guardrail and rolled down the rocky embankment of the raised highway. The SUV landed upside-down. White vapor-smoke poured out from the engine. Rocking, with wheels spinning in the air, Dallas lost consciousness.

7

New Fixation

Dallas woke up under buzzing fluorescent lights. Unable to focus, her eyes could only detect the difference between the blurry color of vanilla custard and the bright shine of stainless steel. Her eyeballs felt dry but didn't hurt. She blinked and felt the momentary relief of darkness, only to return to her yellow haze when her eyes opened. Her mind seemed to be floating in a surreal symphony of mechanical sounds. An occasional solo of pain from a distance accompanied the techno-orchestra of muffled beeps and hums. She tried to move and found her limbs weighed a hundred pounds each. A fuzzy blue apparition appeared over her. It spoke.

"Looky who's awake."

The woman's voice sounded like it came from underwater. Dallas's mind screamed as she tried to speak, but no sound came out. Her mouth, like her sandpaper eyes, felt dry. The added sensation of gumminess made her want to chew. Her tongue stuck to the roof of her mouth, and her jaw fought back when she tried to open it. Dallas felt like she was choking on her teeth.

"Dallas? You're at Kindred Hospital, I'm nurse Donna," the underwater voice said.

She felt a touch on her hand, but her arm did not feel like her own. The azul ghost hovered around her. Liquid coldness flowed into this same disassociated hand. It crept up her arm, toward her center, closer and closer, until it absorbed her warmth. Moments later, her mind sunk back into her body. Her lead limbs felt lighter and lighter with each breath. Except for her right arm—something felt wrong there. The ghost sharpened and focused into an image that Dallas recognized as female. Then a nurse. A nurse in blue scrubs.

"I bet you'd like to whet your whistle," the nurse said as she pushed a button, and the mechanical bed folded upward. Nurse Donna had a thick waist that matched her heavy Southern accent. Both features an unusual find in Las Vegas. Her blond and gray hair gathered in a knot on top of her already abnormally bulbous head.

Dallas managed to turn her head and nod. The nurse aimed a bendy straw into her mouth. And Dallas sipped the most refreshing ice water she had ever tasted in her life. She swallowed a mouthful of glue and tried to speak again.

"Dallas sure's an interestin' name. Were y'all born in Texas, sugah'?"

"No. Football."

"Football?"

"Cowboys. Daddy's team."

"Oh, your dad named y'all for the Dallas Cowboys?

"Yeah."

"So you're a big football fan then?"

"No. I run."

"That's nice I guess."

"What… Happened?"

"Y'all had an automobile accident. A real tumbler," Donna said with a thick southern drawl.

"Don't remember."

"That's the concussion talking. Y'all 'most lost your arm there, sugah'."

Dallas looked down her left arm and only saw the IV dripping into the back of her hand.

"O'er there. Your other arm, punkin'." Nurse Donna pointed.

Dallas looked to her right and saw a mechanical monster attached to her swollen and grotesque arm. Grateful to be numb, she admired the impressive metal rig that held her crushed arm together. Her eyes widened in awe of the mechanics.

"That's called an Ilizarov apparatus," Donna said.

"Ill lizard—"

"Ilizarov, sugah'. Whatcha got there is an external fixator holding your arm in place, so the bones can heal inside."

Dallas attempted to lift her arm and got it an inch off the bed before giving up and dropping it. Even with all the opiates coursing through her blood, the slight impact sent a shockwave of pain through her body.

"Now don't try movin' yet. Your arm got crushed an' nearly amputated right there 'bove your wrist." Nurse Donna gestured over the lower circle of the fixator to show Dallas exactly where. "There's a metal plate inside holdin' your ulna together." She pointed at one-of-five solid stainless steel pins. "These screw right into your bone."

Dallas examined the mechanical structure of her new apparatus. Her engineering mind analyzed the precision hardware. Guide-holes lined two curved pieces of steel alloy. They bolted together to complete a circular, external fixator around her wrist. Another identical circle rig mirrored the first one and rested below her elbow. Bolted thick threaded rods held the armature together. A padded rest supported the palm of her hand. Tracking the steel pins, she picked at the bandages to see where they impaled her dark flesh. Blood oozed out. She imagined the pins screwing into her bones. She tried to picture the way the screws must be anchored into a plate inside. Fascinated, she wanted to take her whole arm apart and study it.

(I coulda been good at this kind of surgery.)

She tinkered with thick nuts and bolts and wished for an adjustable crescent wrench.

(If not for the blood. I hate gore.)

A flashback of her disemboweled dog shot through her eidetic memory. "Damn."

"No more messin' 'roun with that arm," Donna warned.

"Okay, okay."

"No, it's not okay. Y'all 'most lost your arm, sugah'. That could still happen if y'all don't listen up."

"I might lose my arm?" Dallas looked down at the dead, limp limb pinned to her Transformer-like exoskeleton.

"That's right. Y'all gotta whole series of surgeries an' a long road of rehab to save that arm. It's not as cool as y'all think, sugah'. There's a whole lotta work ahead waitin' for y'all."

8

Kite Tails

After spending a few weeks at Kindred Hospital, Dallas felt thrilled to go back to work. She moved slower these days. Getting dressed had been a challenge, since no sleeve in the world would fit over her fixator. She chose a royal-blue, wife-beater tank-top over a sports bra and she had no idea how she would fit into her coveralls at work.

(I can't believe I get to wear this thing for another month.)

Dallas lifted the rig and rotated her arm to admire it. "I'm part machine now." She checked the time. Dallas poked between the blinds to see if the taxi had arrived yet. Instead of a cab, she saw the entire cul-de-sac had been barricaded off by police cars. An ambulance pulled up.

"What the—?"

Dallas dashed outside. Yellow, *Police Line Do Not Cross* tape marked the perimeter of Maricela's property, which buzzed with Metro officers. She recognized Garrison and McCoy. The disturbed expressions on their normally cop-stone faces made her heart race. Dallas skirted the edge of the crime scene, careful to stay behind the line while craning her neck and standing on her tiptoes to catch a glimpse.

When Dallas found a break in the overgrown hedgerow, she saw him. At first, her mind rejected the scene. She shut her eyes, but the horrifying afterimage haunted her. She bent over and vomited in the thick evergreens, as the gory picture burned another scar into her memory forever.

An eight-foot, wrought-iron spike stood erect in Maricela's rose garden right in the center of her front yard. It looked like the kind of spire she'd seen on the top of Gothic cathedrals in horror movies. Thick as a flagpole at the bloody base, the stake tapered into a sharp point. At the bottom, the pole plunged into the deep bed, surrounded by over a dozen prize-winning, hybrid roses. Mounted at the top, the finial's vicious-looking spear-point invoked empathetic pain. That impressive metal skewer had impaled Ramone's rectum, penetrated through his entire nude body, and reappeared out of his mouth.

(Just like Bella.)

Dallas opened her eyes, needing to know what happened to her friend. She examined the gruesome, and yet hauntingly familiar, scene. Ramone's rigor mortised legs held a running pose with one foot on the ground and the other pointing out at a ninety-degree angle toward her. Rope bound Ramone's hands behind his back.

(I'm no detective, but his pose makes we wonder. I can almost picture it. This monster tied Ramone's hands behind his back, and when the kid tried to make a run for it, crammed the wrought iron spear up his ass. How much force would it take to impale a human body lengthwise?)

She struggled to wrap her head around the physics. It helped to intellectualize her feelings this way. She did some math. Then she concluded the muscular strength of one man could never thrust that heavy wrought-iron skewer through a body. Ending her analysis, her empathy returned.

(Poor Ramone.)

Ramone's dead eyes stared up at the morning sun. His raspberry-slushy-blue bangs rustled with the wind. Dallas had a mental flashback to Bella's matching blue fur blowing in the morning breeze. The similarities made her teeth tingle. She fought the urge to puke again and ducked under the police tape to hide in the evergreens. She pushed through the overgrowth a bit, trying to get an even better view.

(Wish I could stop looking. I feel drawn to it—compelled.)

Sticky, crimson blood soaked deep into the mulch surrounding the past-their-peak rose bushes.

(I wondered if Maricela's roses will be even more spectacular next spring.)

Dallas moved to an angle where she could see around Ramone's raised leg. His abdomen had been sliced open, and his internal organs had all been removed and displayed in that recognizable, grisly cascade.

(It's the same killer.)

A crime scene photographer took pictures of every possible gory angle. Another forensic investigator measured the scene. One looked for footprints. Another analyzed blood splatter. And yet another searched for evidence dropped in the yard. An ambulance crew and workers in Coroner jackets waited along the fringe.

(Where's Maricela? Luca? I hope they're okay.)

"Ma'am. You can't be here," a deep voice startled her.

"My friends live there." Dallas jumped back out of the bushes, and her fixator got snarled on a branch. She wiggled her arm like a fox with its paw stuck in a trap.

This gigantic cop stood at least a foot taller than her and held his authoritarian stance. "This is a crime scene, ma'am."

"Ramone used to walk my dog," Dallas said.

(And now he's dead too.)

She jerked her arm again but remained hooked on the tree.

"I said, 'step back,'" the officer commanded, seeming even taller.

Dallas pointed through the shrubbery. "That's Ramone. The one. On the spike." Then she ripped and swatted at the tangled evergreen with her good hand until she finally broke free. Nearly tumbling to the giant's feet, she recovered. "That happened to my dog too. Three weeks ago."

"Your dog?" The behemoth asked, lifting the caution tape for her.

"I live right here." Dallas pointed to her house. Then she ducked back under the police line to return to her side of the law.

The monumental officer pulled out his notepad and clicked a pen. "What's your name?"

"Dallas Mack."

"And your address?"

"Seven-sixty-five Palo Verde Lane." Dallas pointed to her house.

"Were you home last night?"

"Yes. Maricela Nunez, she's Ramone's mom. She's my friend. Maricela came and picked me up from the hospital yesterday." Dallas brandished her busted arm to show him. "Then she dropped me off, and I hung out at home until I went to sleep. I haven't been home all week."

"What time did you get home yesterday?"

"I don't know. Dinner time I guess. Maricela said she needed to make dinner."

"Did you see anything unusual last night?" The towering officer gave her a suspicious look.

"Of course not," Dallas snapped back at him. "I mean, if I had seen anything, don't you think I would have told someone right away?"

The mountainous officer did not respond.

"It's not like Metro did anything when I called last time. My dog got murdered, and you all acted like it was nothing. I still haven't heard anything about Bella's investigation."

"Again about the dog?" The giant cop stopped taking notes.

"Yeah, my dog was killed. Impaled. Just like that." Dallas pointed to her front yard. "It happened about three weeks ago."

"You do understand that a dead dog does not prompt a murder investigation, right? That this—" The colossal officer gestured at the grand, investigative orchestra around them. "Is different?"

"Whoa, whoa. Back it up!" someone yelled from the other side of the evergreen shrubbery.

The reaction of a grumbling crowd followed, demanding everyone's attention. Dallas caught a glimpse. As the crew tried to free the iron stake from the ground, one of the officers slipped in the bloody mud. Then, as if the earth opened up and swallowed her leg, another cop sunk shin deep into the muck. She yanked her foot free with the help of her partner. The officer pulled out her socked foot out of the muck, leaving her shoe underground.

Thwuck.

"It's not gonna give," the officer yelled, defeated. She limped out of the way. "Bring in the lift."

"Let me try," another tech said plugging in his Sawzall at the closest exterior outlet. He eagerly approached the bottom of the pole, revved his saw, and made contact. Within seconds, they all heard a sound that let them know things went wrong.

Whiz, snap, twang.

"Ahhh, wha?" the tech screamed as a broken piece of blade stuck in his thigh. A paramedic swooped in and helped him limp away to the ambulance for treatment.

As if on cue, a hulking yellow crane lumbered toward the scene. The giant interviewer pulled Dallas aside and out of the way. The heavy equipment pushed past the evergreens and hoisted its rig over the impaled body. An old and leathery female grabbed the chain from overhead. She unlatched the hook and forced the links under Ramone's armpits as rigor mortis fought her. Then she finished by latching the chain across his chest. She made a repeating, upward lifting motion with her arm. The crane's engine revved and whined as the winch wound the chain around a spool.

Inch-by-inch, the crane lifted Ramone's body up the spike, leaving a smeary trail of blood and chunks behind on the rough iron. It took forever for the finial to disappear down Ramone's throat. Dallas expected his head to flop forward as it came off the spike, but he stayed frozen in his pose. Ramon's body towered over the crew of onlookers as the crane lifted him higher until his ass slid off the spike. His corpse dangled by the chains as the crane backed away from his house. He glided through the air with his entrails dangling behind him like bloody kite tails.

As Ramone approached overhead, anxiety welled up inside Dallas. The aerial path of the corpse provided a unique photographic image with each passing second. She saw parts of Ramone she never wanted to see. She saw parts of Ramone from angles she never imagined. It burned into her memory. Fixated, Dallas looked up at the nude teenager's eviscerated body. She raised her mechanical contraption of an arm to block the morning sun and the image of Ramone from her eyes.

(Why would anyone want to be a cop? Why would anyone want to see such horrible things?)

A gust blew. And a piece a dark shrapnel flew out of Ramone's abdominal cavity and through the air straight for Dallas. It lodged itself inside her arm's fixator.

Clank.

The officer followed the path of the projectile like a cat focused on a red laser dot.

"What the–?" Dallas said as she examined her fixator.

The broken finial from the top of the spike had attached itself to her rig. It must have broken loose when Ramone's body slid over it. Dallas poked at the bloody piece of wrought iron with her good hand.

"You can't take that. It's evidence," the giant cop said.

(Cut me a break, man.)

"I didn't take it." Dallas tried to pry the spear tip free from the long rod of her fixator.

"Hand it over."

"I'm trying," Dallas replied, offering her arm to him so that he could pull it free. The officer tried to muscle the bloody finial free but had no success either.

"It's stuck."

Once in the street, the crane lowered the body onto the Coroner's gurney. An EMT cut the bindings around

Ramones wrists. Then two more techs joined to help lay him flat inside a body bag. The emergency techs fought with Ramone's stiff limbs, trying to get them straight. The sound of cracking and popping made Dallas want to barf again. Finally, a female medic zipped the body bag shut over Ramone's face and rolled him away.

Maricela broke through the front door, stormed straight through the crime scene, and raced after her son. The medical crew and gurney rolled past Dallas and headed for the Coroners van instead of the ambulance.

"Hold on there," the giant said, abandoning Dallas to strong-arm Maricela.

"*Mi hijo*," Maricela cried.

"You can't go with him right now."

"Why not?"

"Because he's evidence, ma'am."

Dallas shot the officer a nasty look and put her arm around her friend. "He's still her son."

(Asshole!)

The officer stood firm and blocked the women as the crew slammed the back doors of the Coroner's van. It drove away, and Maricela sobbed uncontrollably. Dallas held her friend as Maricela collapsed into her arms. Tears flowed onto Dallas's shoulder.

"Oh, Maricela. I'm so sorry," Dallas said, hiding the gory piece of metal stuck to her arm behind her back.

"*Mi hijo*," Maricela cried so hard that she had to breathe through sobs.

"What happened?"

"After I brought you home from *el hospital*. We ate dinner, *vío la television*, and went to bed." Maricela always slipped into Spanglish when upset.

"Then what?"

"*No lo sé*… Ramone didn't come down for breakfast. I couldn't find him. I pinged his phone and followed the signal. And then I found him. *Jodido como esa*. Fucked. Like that," Maricela said, pleading into her friend's eyes and gesturing toward the bloody spike that still stood erected in her yard.

Dallas caught the cop staring at them, taking notes. She pulled Maricela away and whispered in her ear, "I promise you. I'm going to find the monster who did this."

Maricela sobbed even harder. Dallas put her arm around her friend and shot the cop a *stay-back* glance. "These cops. They don't give a fuck about people like us."

Luca appeared. Maricela released a fresh round of tears at the sight of her husband. Luca pulled Maricela away from her friend and shot Dallas a nasty look. Dallas stopped hiding her arm. The gooey finial fell from her fixator and hit the asphalt.

Clang, ting, clang, clang.

The giant cop dove for the evidence and snatched it.

The pipe clenched in his teeth wiggled up and down when Luca talked. "Come now." He guided his wife back to their house.

Feeling like a third wheel, Dallas abandoned the cop and followed her friends.

"This for family," Luca declared. He snarled at Dallas while blowing smoke at her. Luca whisked Maricela back into their house. A Team of police officers awaited them.

Dallas took a step backward and found herself closer to the cop bagging evidence. Her taxi rolled up in front of her house in time to save her from more questions. The cab blasted its horn.

Honk, honk.

"Time to go to work," Dallas muttered nervously to the cop, as she scuttled away. At first, she reached for the car door with her injured hand. Then she lowered her broken arm, turned to her weaker side, and used her left to open the door. Everything felt so much harder now.

(Takes so much more effort.)

Dallas hopped into the backseat of the cab and reached across herself to yank the door shut.

"Hoover Dam please," she said to the driver.

"This is some mess, huh?" the driver asked, gesturing to the crime scene beyond his dashboard.

"Sure is," she agreed, fumbling with the seatbelt.

"Too many sickos in this world." The driver shook his head.

"I'm gonna stop the motherfucker who did this, even if it kills me." Dallas tossed the buckle aside and rested her fixator on her lap.

"Who you?" The driver looked at his rearview mirror. "You're all broken. What are you gonna do?"

"Just what I said," Dallas said with determination. "'I'm gonna stop the motherfucker.'"

9

Dangerous Wake

Dallas ignored the dead body on the over-garnished altar in Maricela's dining room. She chose to stare down at her styrofoam plate of Mexican food instead, as she sat alone in the corner of the cramped eat-in kitchen. Representatives from both the Nunez and Rosales family circled the oak table to fill their plates from the wake's potluck buffet. Dallas had selected carne asada and tamales with fresh, homemade guacamole.

(Smells delicious. But this ambiance killed my appetite long ago.)

Her red solo cup of sangria sat on the floor by her suede ankle-boots. She poked at the tamale's husk, then peeled thin strips away bit-by-bit until she created an impressive cornhusk tassel. Then she fiddled with the knitted yarn of her ice-blue short sleeve sweater dress—the only dress in her entire wardrobe.

(Stupid dress. I should have worn black, but nothing fit over this fixator.)

Dallas had never been to a Mexican wake before. The surreal and gruesome impalement yesterday seemed like they had happened a lifetime ago. And nothing could have prepared her for the awkward culture shock of this evening. Yesterday, despite speaking almost no English, Luca had gone downtown and fought to get Ramone back so the family could mourn in the traditional Mexican way. Thanks to his stepfather's persistence, Ramone's body had been autopsied and returned in record time. Maricela had wrapped his embalmed and stitched remains in a burial shroud and displayed him in the traditional coffin sleeping position on her dining room table. Except there was no coffin. Ramone's corpse laid flat on the same table where they had gathered to eat dinner and play *Scrabble* every Tuesday night.

(Won't be doing that ever again.)

Engracia Nunez, a frail woman in her mid-eighties, rested her cane against the refrigerator. After fumbling with styrofoam edges for a minute or so, she freed the top plate from the thick stack. Her gnarly hand shook as it scooped refried beans into an indented food well. She added homemade salsa. When the old lady reached for a flour tortilla, her plate tilted at such an extreme angle that all the beans nearly slid off. Dallas hopped up, left her plate on her chair, and assisted by supporting the grandmother's plate from beneath.

"Let me help you."

"*¿Qué?*" Engracia asked.

"*Lo hago,*" Dallas said.

(Did I say, 'I'll do it' right? I suck at Spanish.)

The senior woman smiled, and her dentures slipped. Neither of them cared. Dallas pulled a steaming tortilla from the warmer with her gimpy fixator hand, rolled it up, and placed it on the plate for the grandmother. Then Engracia retrieved her cane and Yoda-walked back through the kitchen. Dallas followed her into the living room where the rest of the family elders sat and ate together in silence. The grandmother chose the high-backed armchair next to the glittery gold and red Christmas tree in the corner. She sat. Engracia's brother selected the last TV tray from a rack and set it in front of his sister. Dallas placed the woman's food on the tray.

"*Gracias,*" the old lady said, settling in to eat.

"*De nada,*" Dallas replied.

The elders gawked at her fixator. Some seemed impressed, others seemed frightened, but no one spoke. Feeling like the oddball, Dallas decided to exit. She backed out of the room while announcing, "It's time I paid my respects to Ramone."

She detoured through the hallway and froze before stepping into the dining room. Funeral flowers sent by family and friends covered every inch of wall space. Golden-glittered expressions of sympathy written across ribbon banners draped each floral arrangement, all in Spanish. The long mahogany dining room table rested against the longest wall–the one with the king-sized crucifix. Stretching from wall to wall, a garland of palm leaves, citrus fruit, and orange flowers formed a massive arch over the burial table. Dozens of lit prayer candles featuring images of Jesus, the Virgin Mary, and other Holy Saints lined the edge.

(*I swear, I will never eat at that table again.*)

Standing as far away as possible, the scent of flowers, citrus, candles, and Mexican food mixed with Luca's ever-present cherry tobacco smoke. Reminding her of an armed guard, Luca stood by his stepson in silence. Nagging necrophobia made Dallas want to bolt. She imagined running to the safety of her home. And the movie memory of burying Bella's dead body played in her mind.

(I survived that somehow. I can do this.)

"But people are worse," she whispered to herself.

Dallas recalled her father's funeral. Only six-years-old at his viewing, she held her mother's hand while gazing up at the looming casket. Then suddenly, her mom let go and launched herself headlong over the high ledge. The crying and sobbing and wailing made Dallas worry. Not being able to see what caused her mom so much pain, paralyzed Dallas with fear. All of the sudden, without a word or warning, her mother turned and lifted her daughter over the open coffin.

"Say good-bye to Daddy," her mother cried hysterically.

The man in the casket looked like her father, but at the same time, did not. Never having seen a dead person before, Dallas expected him to be—normal.

(But Daddy was pretty damn far from normal.)

"Give him a kiss," her mother instructed, tipping her daughter's head downward.

Hovering over her daddy with her face inches from his, Dallas felt utterly powerless. Forced to remember her father's dead face up close and out of focus, overwhelmed her child-mind. She wiggled to push away as her mom lowered her closer and closer. Something looked wrong. Color. Something smelled wrong. Perfume. Something felt wrong. Cold. Dallas freaked out. She kicked and screamed and flailed. And then the most horrible thing happened.

(Momma dropped me. In the casket with Daddy.)

Her breaths came quicker, more shallow. Sweat dripped down the back of her neck. Her fists clenched.

(Haven't touched a dead body since.)

Now Ramone laid in front of her. Dead. From her point of view, Dallas could see Ramone's altar and the Christmas tree in the next room at the same time. The bizarre juxtaposition of images baffled her brain. She resisted what came next. She didn't know if she could do it. Her thought-paralyzed zen place seemed safe, and she wanted to stay there. Instead, she forced herself to take one step forward, hoping that viewing Ramone would push the last gory image of him out of her head forever.

"You come," Luca said to Dallas, making a come-here gesture. "You friend. Come."

(Oh, thank God. He broke the ice.)

Dallas approached Luca while avoiding the altar.

"I'm sorry for your loss." She cringed at the trite words as she held out her right hand to shake.

Luca gently accepted the gesture, careful not to bump her fixator and hurt her. He let Dallas control the grip and the up and down movement of their handshake.

"Why you sorry?" Luca asked. "Not you fault. You good friend."

Maricela appeared from the kitchen to join them. As soon as she stood within arms reach of the table, Maricela grabbed and caressed her son's wrapped, cold, dead hand. Dallas forced herself to look at Ramone—to remember. The family had bundled him in a gauzy burial shroud that made him resemble a clean mummy. Several layers of fabric made it impossible to see his abdominal butchering underneath. Dallas wondered if the Coroner had shoved his organs back inside and then stitched him closed. Then she wondered if the family had to do that instead. Either way, Ramone looked complete. Solid.

With only one thin layer over Ramone's head, his raspberry-blue hair showed through the loose weave. All the other color had faded from his face.

(He's so pale. Lifeless.)

Maricela held a death grip on her son. Dallas put her hand on her grieving friend's shoulder. Tears welled up in both women's eyes, but this time, there was no sobbing.

(Just silence.)

Dallas didn't know Luca well. He'd only been with Maricela a year or so, and the language barrier hindered communication. But today, Dallas saw a new side of him. He stood strong for his wife, and at the same time; Dallas witnessed his soft side. Then the doorbell rang.

"Pardon," Luca said as he left the ladies at the altar to greet the guest at the front door.

A short, stocky Latino man named Samuel Rosales stormed up to the altar with Luca trailing close behind. His face red with anger, Samuel spat vicious words at Maricela, "This is your fault, you *puta loca!* My only son is dead because of you."

Maricela released her grip, and Ramone's hand stuck stiffly over the edge of the table. She turned to face her ex-husband. "You smell like a brewery, Samuel."

(I don't smell any alcohol.)

Luca caught up with the intrusive mourner and stepped in front of his wife. "You respect! No talk such way."

Samuel got up in Luca's face. "Whatcha gonna do about it, *jefe?*"

Luca pulled his pipe from his mouth. "Tread careful."

"Is that some kind of threat?" Samuel asked, puffing himself up.

The men stood nose-to-nose. Then Luca, to no one's surprise, blew smoke right into Samuel's face before biting the pipe between his teeth again. Sensing trouble brewing, Dallas stepped back from the fighting men. Her backside bumped against Ramone's hand.

(What the hell?)

Mortified, Dallas jumped forward and bumped into Maricela. Like falling dominos, Maricela bumped into Luca, who accidentally lunged forward. In his aggravated state, Samuel read Luca's move as an attack.

Samuel swung the first punch. He landed a right hook firmly on Luca's jaw, knocking the pipe out of his mouth. The one-of-a-kind antique piece flew across the room and hit the wall. Then tobacco and sparks sprayed through the air as the pipe bounced on the hardwood floor. Seeing his most prized possession crash to the ground enraged Luca. He charged at Samuel.

The two men brawled, punched, and kicked. Out of instinct, Maricela dashed out of the room. But Dallas stood frozen, overwhelmed by disbelief of the surreal tragedy unfolding around her. The men fought back and forth with no clear winner for several minutes. Luca split Samuel's lip. Then Samuel delivered a gut punch that sent Luca reeling backward. Luca fell, splayed across the funeral table. His momentum slid Ramone right off the edge. Onlookers gasped and cried aloud from the next room.

Without thinking, Dallas dove to catch the falling body before it hit the floor, but she underestimated Ramone's dead weight. The corpse tumbled to the ground, and Dallas fell into a pile with it. Several bolts of her fixator snagged the gauze of the burial shroud. She yanked her arm free, but tore the dressing off Ramone's body instead.

(Shit! It's touching me. Get off!)

Dallas kicked and screamed bloody murder to get that dead body away from her. In the processes, she unwound Ramone's burial dressing and kicked open his sloppily stitched abdominal cavity.

Still trapped under the weight of the corpse, Dallas flailed and kicked and screamed like someone drowning.

Intestines, vital organs, and a few not-so-vital ones spilled out of the remains and onto Dallas making her even more manic. During her full blown panic attack, Ramone's embalmed, but still slimy, liver fell onto her face. It slid down into the crook of her neck.

"Fuck!" she screamed, tearing at the organ with her nails.

Dallas clenched the gooey thing and threw it high across the room to get it off her. The slippy organ launched across the room. Everyone gaped in disbelief. And then the liver flew right for a Metro officer who had just walked into the wake. The slick liver hit the cop in the face with a splat.

A whole house of mortified mourners witnessed the incident. Even Luca and Samuel stopped fighting and gawked at Dallas. Panting and gasping in terror, Dallas crawled out from under Ramone with his gauze still hooked onto her fixator. When she came up for air, she recognized the gigantic cop as the one that had interviewed her the day before. He frowned at her, holding Ramone's liver in his gargantuan hand.

Not amused, the officer marched across the dining room, ducked under the spinning three blades of the ceiling fan, and smacked the liver onto the table.

Splat.

The cop offered Dallas a hand up. She took hold with her left as he helped her to her feet.

"Dallas Mack, you're under arrest," the offended giant said, pulling out his handcuffs.

(Dammit.)

"Of course I am," Dallas said, defeated. She presented both her wrists to him.

The huge officer considered the complicated contraption on her left arm and rejected the idea of cuffing it. The tattered end of Ramone's burial shroud remained caught on her hardware and billowed down to the corpse on the floor. Tugging at the cloth perfectly, it tore free, and the policeman let the gauze flutter to his feet. Not wanting to touch her hardware again, the cop cuffed her left wrist. The other bracelet jetted out of his hand and stuck to the metal circle of her external fixator. The cop tried to pry the cuff free, but he failed.

"Is that some sort of magnet?" he asked.

"I don't know," Dallas said.

"Guess that'll hold you," the cop said. "Don't give me any trouble. Okay, Dallas?"

"I get into more trouble when trying not to make trouble," she said as the officer escorted her out of Maricela's house, through the suburban night, and finally into the back of his squad car. The humungous cop drove her downtown to jail.

(Just another Tuesday night at Maricela's house.)

10

∩

Turbo Fiesta

"Fuck the police," Dallas barked as she walked out of the Clark County Detention Center. "I'm a free woman," she screamed up at the night sky. Hopping down the concrete steps and across the sidewalk, she felt lighter—unburdened. Getting arrested flipped a switch inside her.

(I've always been such a good girl.)

When the tangerine Ford Fiesta Turbo rolled up, she skipped to the tinted window and smiled. The passenger window rolled down revealing Clark's grining face.

"Get in, Mack." He gestured to the seat behind him.

Dallas opened the little rear door with her left hand, jumped inside, and reached across herself to slam it shut behind her. Her knees crammed into the back of Clark's seat. The same height as her, he had reclined and slid the seat back as far as it could go. Dallas hunched over to keep her head from hitting the roof and wrapped her arms around her knees. Todd sat next to her in the back and smiled as he watched her sweater dress ride up her thigh. Being modest, Dallas tugged and stretched the knit while shooting Todd a back-off look.

"I love dark chocolate," Todd said, admiring her long legs and leaning over the centerline.

"Fuck you, carrot top." Dallas pushed him back.

"Fuck me? Why?"

"Didn't your momma teach you it's rude to use food to describe the color of a person's skin?"

"How's dark chocolate an insult? It's delicious." Todd gave her a suggestive look.

"Is ginger an insult?" Dallas flicked his curly hair with her finger.

"I don't know," Todd answered honestly.

"Trust me. It's not a compliment." Dallas crossed her arms.

"Tough night?" Clark turned to face the back seat.

"Never been arrested before," Dallas said. She tapped Steve on the shoulder. "Don't go anywhere yet. You hear me, do NOT drive." Then she turned to Clark. "It's your turn to be back here."

"No chance, Mack. I've declared perma-shotgun. What'd you do to get locked up anyway?"

"They charged me with *Assaulting a Police Officer*."

"Wow." Todd ogled her.

"You hit a cop?" Clark asked.

"No. I threw—I accidentally threw something at a cop." Dallas stretched her skirt down over her knees.

"Poor Dallas," Steve said from behind the wheel.

"Don't say that," Dallas snapped as she fiddled with her fixator. "I'm not poor. I'm no victim. Do not pity me. I don't want your pity."

"Are we going anywhere?" Steve asked, checking his white hair in the rearview mirror. "Or should we hang out here in the jail parking lot getting yelled at all night?"

Todd yawned, stretched, and rested his arm across the top of the backseat. His hand waited on her headrest for the perfect opportunity.

"If you touch me, Todd, I swear I will break your hand so bad that you'll need one of these." Dallas swished her fixator toward him.

Todd withdrew his arm and sat on his hands.

"You know what, Clark? Get out. I'm riding shotgun." Dallas popped her door open.

"What? But I always ride shotgun."

"Not this time, buddy." Her right shoe hit the pavement.

"But I'm too tall to sit in the back."

"I'm exactly as tall as you," Dallas argued. "And I'm not playing with Mr. Ginger Grabby Hands anymore." Dallas jumped out of the backseat and then opened his door for him. "Out big guy. Move it, Clark."

Clark sighed and released his seat belt. Then he trudged to the backseat. Dallas took her rightful place in the front. They slammed their doors shut in unison.

"Holy Chinese fire drill, Batman," Steve said.

"Chinese?" Her stomach growled. "Hey, you guys up for grabbing some food? It's after ten, and I haven't eaten since lunch."

"Sure what's open?" Steve asked. "Wanna hit a drive thru?"

"No. Chinese sounded great," Dallas said. "Let's go to the cafe at South Point."

Steve checked the rearview. The guys smiled back at him, so he stomped the gas and peeled out. "Ha, ha! Turbo, bitches!"

"This is the county jail, Steve. There are cops everywhere. We'll get pulled over," Clark said, leaning through the bucket seats.

"Who cares what cops think?" Dallas laughed. It was the first time she had smiled all day. She turned to Steve and joked, "so this tangerine economy hatchback is a turbo? A turbo Fiesta? Seriously?"

Steve nodded with pride while driving. "Yes, except it's safety-orange. Thank you very much."

"Aren't these things only three cylinders?" Dallas asked as they sped through a yellow light.

"Yup." Steve nodded.

"A three-cylinder turbo?" Dallas laughed, petting the dashboard.

"Yup, and I get thirty-three miles to the gallon."

"I'm sorry, but that's the stupidest thing I've ever heard in my life," Dallas giggled.

"Says the woman with no car of her own," Steve snipped, annoyed.

"All right, if you say so," Dallas said. "Hey, thanks for picking me up guys. I've had a nightmare of a night, and I appreciate it."

"No problem," Steve said.

"Yeah we were just playing *Fallout 4*," Clark said from the back seat.

"Well, I was the one playing. I killed a death claw right before you called," Todd said. "These guys just watched,"

"It's been rough getting around since the accident." Dallas shook her fixator. "I'm still waiting for my settlement check from the insurance company. Till then, no car for me."

"You can count on us, Mack," Steve said.

"So how much longer do you gotta wear that thing?" Clark pointed at her fixator.

"A while. I have another surgery after Christmas."

"So, Mack, have you taken it apart yet?" Steve asked.

"This?" She turned and held the mechanical rig out for him. "You know me. I've tweaked it a bit."

All *Three Amigos* laughed.

"Gotta make improvements, right?" Clark asked.

Dallas nodded. "You know what's strange? It seems to be magnetic."

"Magnetic?" Clark popped his head between the seats like an eager gopher. "Let me see."

Dallas twisted as far as she could to give Clark a look at the fixator.

"That's an alloy. It shouldn't be magnetic," Clark said while tapping the metal.

"Well, it attracts metal stuff."

"What kind of stuff?" Clark asked.

"Metal stuff. Like I said."

"Clark has a magnet fixation," Steve explained.

"True. Let's talk about magnets." Clark's head disappeared from the front seat as quickly as it reappeared. He spun around and hung over the back seat, diving into the hatchback. He rustled around in the cargo area and appeared with an aluminum briefcase, the kind that spies carry in the movies. "Okay, I've got my gear, let's check this thing out."

11

⌒

Iron Filings

Then the engineers stepped onto the casino floor, unloaded from the elevator, and hiked through banks of slot machines before walking up to the *Coronado Cafe* register. A tired-looking hostess seated them in a half-circle booth. Dallas slid in first and scooted the whole way around, then Clark, then Steve, then Todd. The unremarkable hostess placed a laminated menu the size of a newspaper in front of each of them before walking away without a word.

Without opening her menu, Dallas pushed it aside. "I know what I want."

Steve put his on top of hers. "Me too."

Clark and Todd opened their menus and buried their faces inside, studying the offerings.

A half-alive skeleton with breast implants and a bad bleach job walked up to the table. "Can I get your drinks?"

Dallas asked, "Hey guys, are you ready to order? 'Cause I'm starving."

Clark nodded, folded his menu, and added it to the stack. Todd peeked over the top of his, then disappeared again.

Dallas continued without him. "I'll have an order of pot stickers and the firecracker chicken, as hot as you can make it." She smiled and paused, then pointed firmly at the table to emphasize what she said next, "I mean hot. On a scale of one to ten, with ten being a nuclear blast. I want eleven. Understand?"

The waitress scribbled the order on her pad. "Hot. Got it. Something to drink?"

"Just water," Dallas said.

"I'll have the meatloaf special and a Coke," Clark said.

"Pepsi all right?" the waitress asked.

"Not really. But I'll drink it."

"I'll have the three amigos burrito," Steve said.

Dallas laughed out loud.

"What?" Steve asked.

"Nothing," Dallas giggled.

"And orange juice," Steve added.

The waitress gathered up the menus. Everyone stared in Todd's direction, awaiting his decision.

"I'll have a bowl of Fruit Loops and a Pepsi."

The entire table paused for a second. No one wanted to bother making a comment about Todd's choice. But Dallas snatched a menu from the waitress, scanned it, and spoke up.

"Wait, Todd. You're gonna pay $4.95 for a bowl of Fruit Loops?" She pointed at the price and held it up for him to see.

"He always does," Steve said.

"Thank you, Steve. But I want to hear from Todd," Dallas dismissed the interruption. "Why on earth would you spend five dollars for a bowl of cereal?"

"It's what I like."

"But you realize, you could buy a whole box of Fruit Loops for five bucks, right?" Dallas handed the menu back to the waitress.

Todd shrugged.

"Bring the guy his cereal," Steve said to the bored waitress.

She walked away with their orders, and Clark whipped out his spy briefcase, slid it onto the table, and cracked it open. Clark's hand glided, palm side up, over the contents of the case like a spokesmodel showing off a shiny new car on a game show. Organized tools loaded the top compartment, with each neatly stashed away in its own spot. Screwdrivers, Allen wrenches, adjustable wrenches, and a variety of pliers, lined up by descending size from left to right. In the bottom of the case, custom carved compartments held button, ring, sphere, cube, bar, and horseshoe magnets. Each magnet fit securely into the foam. Clark lifted the clear acrylic divider that held them all in place and slid it into the pocket behind the tools in the lid.

"That's all kinds of serious, Clark." Dallas gazed into the case.

"It's kinda my thing." Clark took a stack of button magnets stuck together like a roll of thick nickels and handed them to Todd.

The eager redhead took the magnets and tore them apart. He placed them on the table and started pushing them toward each other until they slammed together. Todd snickered to himself. The waitress returned with their drinks and gave the briefcase a funny look as she distributed their glasses. She left without a word.

"He's got money for this kit, but when I ask him to chip in for gas, he's broke," Steve commented, disinterested. He ripped open his straw and sucked down half his orange juice.

"Captain Ed Hardy here is bitching about money," Clark said. "So Mack, pop that puppy up here." Clark patted the tabletop between them. "And tell me why you think your gizmo is magnetic."

Dallas sat her fixator on the table top. All *Three Amigos* leaned in to examine it.

"It's called an—" She paused to recall the correct pronunciation, "Ilizarov apparatus."

"May I?" Clark asked. Then he poked at the long threaded rod.

"Sure. It doesn't hurt," Dallas continued. "So, twice now, it's stuck to things. Metal things. When I got arrested, it stuck to the handcuffs. Before that, a piece of broken wrought iron attached to it."

"Well, this is a regular old threaded rod. It could become magnetized easily enough," Clark said examining her rig. "All it takes is stroking it with another magnet."

"Well that didn't happen," Dallas said.

"Or prolonged contact with another strong magnet?"

"That didn't happen either, Clark."

Clark took the silverware from his place setting. He touched the fork and knife together then pulled them apart with no effort. "Restaurant silverware is not magnetized." He pulled a big bar magnet from his case. "But it can *become* magnetized." Clark rubbed the blue end of the bar magnet down the blade of the knife, lifted it and started at the handle again. He repeated this motion over and over as he spoke, "Many restaurants put magnets in their garbage cans because the busboys keep trashing the silverware by mistake. If a dirty fork sticks to the side of a garbage can long enough, it will become magnetized." Clark stopped stroking the magnet against the knife. He held it to the fork, and they stuck together this time. "Wah-la!"

Steve yawned. "We work on turbines all day, dude. We know how magnets work."

Clark gave Steve the finger, then stole his spoon. He touched his spoon with his own to prove there was no magnetism. Then he touched one to her fixator. Clark let go, and the spoon stuck.

"Whoa," Dallas said.

Suddenly Steve's interest peaked. "So it is magnetic." Steve plucked a bunch of different magnets from the case and stuck them all over her mechanical frame.

"That doesn't prove anything, dumbass. They'd stick to almost any metal," Clark said.

The waitress appeared with a big tray of food and dealt dishes to her guests. Clark pulled his paper placemat away and shoved it in his case. He closed and sat it in the booth between him and Steve. The waitress finished with Dallas, considering her arm and all the crap stuck to it. "Can I get you all anything else?"

"Nope, we're good," Steve spoke for the entire table.

Dallas dug into her food, shoveling. Todd tore a hole in his mini box of cereal and dumped the colorful rings into a bowl, then poured a short glass of milk over them. He ate with dainty table manners. The table fell silent. Halfway through his food and no longer hungry, Clark moved his dishes to the edge of the table. He cracked out his magnet kit again. Dallas ate with both hands, as Clark picked magnets off her fixator and put them back in their cozy case.

"Can I try something, Mack?"

"Sure."

"I need you to hold this still." Clark gestured to her fixator.

Dallas switched to eating pot stickers with her left hand. She rested her arm on the table for him without a word.

Clark took the paper placemat and draped it over her arm. Then he selected a jar of iron filings from his case. He unscrewed the lid and sprinkled it over the paper. Instead of sliding down off her arm, the filings stuck. They formed a rainbow pattern across the paper. He sprinkled more on the other side of her arm, and another rainbow mirrored the first. The ends touched near her elbow and wrist. Clark lifted the paper to look underneath. "Fascinating. The magnetic poles line up with the terminal pins in your arm."

Dallas stopped eating to examine the experiment. "Are those the lines of force?"

"I believe so."

They all huddled around her arm. Clark wiggled the paper, and the iron filing stood up on their ends, looking like small splinters. Steve poked at the concentrated poles by her wrist. They whispered and speculated.

"Excuse me," a deep voice interrupted. A fat security guard stood next to their nervous waitress. "You can't do—whatever you're doing, here."

"They're just iron filings," Clark said.

"It looks like gun powder to me," the waitress said.

"Someone's talking her way out of a tip," Steve said.

"You know what, guys? Let's just go," Dallas said, dropping forty bucks on the table.

Pause.

[And that brings me back to the beginning. To the Pick-A-Part. Because the next night, I disposed of my wrecked Subaru and picked up some parts for a motorcycle I'd been

building with Clark. Just an ordinary errand. Another item to check off my TO DO list. Until it all went sideways.]

12

Seizure Deceiver

(Will he pursue? Where to go? Home? He lives next door.)

Dallas sprinted again. Her mind screamed. Her lungs burned.

(Move. Move. Run! Don't give him time to catch you.)

Instinctively, she ran toward home. A mile passed. Thoughts raced with her.

(He'll come home sooner or later. What to do then? Tell Maricela? Lock my doors and hope? Can't live like that, not day after day. How the hell to deal with this guy? The police. Go to the police. They'll help. Luca needs to be locked up. God, who knows how often he's done this before. But.)

Dallas looked down at her blood-drenched shirt. Her heart hammered in her chest.

(His blood. It's Luca's blood. What if they blame me? I could end up in jail again.)

She ran and ran and ran for miles and didn't stop until she saw the end of her driveway. Before she made it to her porch, she heard Maricela calling her name.

"Dallas? Dallas. Wait a minute."

Still amped up and not ready to talk, Dallas walked faster while looking casual. She pretended not to hear and made a bee-line for her front door, hoping to avoid the inevitable.

"Dallas? Hold up," Maricela yelled running after her.

Dallas stopped, took a deep breath, and turned to face her approaching friend.

"Whoa? What the devil happened to you?" Maricela stopped in her tracks when she saw all the blood.

"It's been a rough night."

"Are you hurt?"

"No. I'm fine."

"*Sangre*. But that's so much blood. Where did all that blood come from?"

(Quick. Make something up.)

"Someone hit a dog with their car." Dallas pointed down the street. "I tried to help."

Maricela looked at her mouth. "With your face?"

(Fuck.)

"Uh, I had to give it mouth to mouth… It didn't make it."

(Damn. I suck at lying.)

"Oh. Yuck. That's too bad. Say, have you seen Luca?"

(Here we go.)

"Why do you ask?"

"He texted me a few hours ago and said you were heading over to the *Pick-A-Part* and that he'd be coming home right after. But… Well, now you're here and he isn't. I haven't heard from him since."

"I stopped by the junkyard to finalize the salvage on my Subaru."

"Luca should have been home by now. What time did you leave?"

"I don't know. An hour ago, maybe."

"Oh my, I hope he's all right," Maricela sighed.

"I'm sure he's fine."

"I worry about him working there alone at night."

"He's a tough guy, Maricela. He can take care of himself."

"Yeah, but he doesn't know Vegas, the way we know Vegas. You know?"

"I can't believe you're worried about him," Dallas mumbled despite herself.

"He's my husband. *Mi esposo*. Of course I worry."

"He's not the guy you think he is, Maricela."

"What are you talking about?"

"Do you want to come inside and talk about it?"

"No. I think you need to explain right now, *amiga*."

"How long have we been friends now?" Dallas asked, digging through her pocket for her keys. "Seven? Eight years?"

"About that long," Maricela said crossing her arms.

(Fuck it.)

Dallas gestured to the blood on her shirt. "Luca attacked me tonight, Maricela. How about that? He locked me in the caboose, threw me down in the bunk, and kissed me."

"I don't believe you."

Dallas pointed to her face. "Look at this. All this is *his* blood. Luca's blood. I bit him. I bit his tongue off!"

"Lies!"

Dallas grabbed her friend by the shoulders and shook her. "Listen to me."

"Take. Your hands. Off me," Maricela said in a slow pace and flat tone.

Dallas relaxed her grip, dropped her arms, and took two steps back. "Maricela, come on. Why would I lie to you."

"You're jealous. You want my man."

"Maricela?"

"You're a home wrecker. Always happy being the other woman. And now without Silver, you're looking to make a move on my Luca. He's an honest man. He's a loving provider. And he has no interest in your skanky ass!" Marcela's phone dinged. She stopped to look. The text came from Luca.

"Had seizure," his text said.

Maricela held it up in her friend's face. "Look. See?"

Dallas read the message. "He's lying, Maricela."

Another message came in. This time it was a photo of Luca in the ER sticking out his swollen and stitched tongue-stub. He added the text, "bit tongue."

"Jesus, I gotta go to the hospital." Maricela broke away from the conversation.

"Coming home now," Luca texted before his wife had a chance to go anywhere.

Maricela tapped back frantically on her phone.

"Maricela," Dallas said.

Her friend ignored her and kept thumb typing.

"Maricela?" Dallas tried again, "Maricela! Look at me."

"What?" She pushed send and looked at her friend.

"He didn't have a seizure."

"What are you talking about?"

"He didn't have a seizure. He didn't bite his own tongue." Dallas gestured to her bloody mess. "I bit off his tongue."

"You're ridiculous. *Estás loca*. You're crazy."

"Then how'd he get those bruises and the cut on his face?"

Maricela looked more closely at the picture. "How'd you know about that?"

"How'd I know he had no tongue? Huh? Think about it." Dallas paused. "He attacked me, and I fought him."

"No. He probably bumped his head when he had the seizure."

"He kissed me, Marcela. He threw me on the bed, and he kissed me. And when he shoved his tongue in my mouth. I bit it off. I bit it right the fuck off. And then I spit it in his fucking face."

"What is wrong with you?"

"Luca is a monster. He got what he deserved."

"No. I mean what happened to make you so… Broken? *Roto*. It's so pathetic that you make up stories for attention. Why can't you be normal like everyone else?"

"Luca is pretty fucking far from normal, Maricela."

Maricela walked up to her friend and stood nose-to-nose with her. She poked her in the chest. "*Tú!*" Maricela held her finger in place, cramming her manicure into her neighbor's sternum. "You, are no longer welcome *en mi casa*. You stay away!"

"Your home is the last place I ever want to be again!"

"*Bueno,*" Maricela snorted as she turned and marched away.

13

∩

Gratuitous Coffin

Still irritated from fighting Luca and arguing with Maricela, Dallas suffered from a killer case of insomnia. She'd spent the last five hours tossing and turning as sleep eluded her. She looked at her phone.

(Push the button. 6 A. M.)

With closed eyes, Dallas did the simple but disappointing math, in about an hour she'd have to leave for work. Frustrated, she opened her eyes and gazed at the streetlight bouncing off the olive branches blowing in the breeze. As much as she hated getting up before her alarm, she knew she wouldn't catch any sleep. And she'd had enough tossing.

(Might as well get up.)

A red glow crept through her blinds. It started subtly but grew in intensity until red light flooded her bedroom. Dallas hopped out of bed and peeked out her window. The light came from Maricela's house, specifically, from her dining room.

"That damn dining room," Dallas muttered.

A strobing, white light interrupted the red flood, accompanied by a blood-curdling scream. Dallas grabbed her phone, ran downstairs, and stepped into her flip-flops. She grabbed her keys and dashed outside in her pajamas to investigate. Navigating the landscape rock in her cheap sandals proved challenging. Halfway across her yard, she wished she had spent a few extra seconds putting on real shoes. She found the narrow gap in the hedgerow and pushed through to her neighbor's yard. Ramon's spike still stood in the front yard like a naked flagpole, but his blood had been washed away days ago.

Dallas tiptoed the best she could in her flimsy shoes and crept up onto her neighbor's porch. She ducked below the dining room window and raised her head high enough to peek through the bottom slat of the almost closed vertical blinds.

(Ramone's funeral altar? Gone.)

The room sat empty except for a shiny, ornately decorated coffin resting on a support scaffolding. She caught a glimpse of Luca from the back. The strobe lights staggered his movement as he held his arms out wide at his sides.

(What the hell are you doing now?)

Dallas reached into the pocket of her flannel pajamas and pulled out her phone. She switched it into silent mode so that her morning alarm wouldn't give her away. She opened the video app, pushed the red button, and recorded Luca. In profile, his sharp facial features and pipe cast a grotesque shadow on the wall.

The ceiling fan spun over his head, stuttering with the strobe light creating a visual effect that disoriented her. The fan wobbled. Three different ancient swords had been crammed into the central mechanism. One, an Ottoman curved, barbed sword called a kilij, she recognized it from watching Todd play *Assassin's Creed*. Another, thin, straight and skinny one, she remembered from *Western Civ II* class as the kind Spanish conquistadors carried. And the third sword, a hybrid of the other two, she could not identify.

Impaled on the family crucifix, a nude female body hovered into the camera's frame. Dallas could not see a face. The enormous cross had been turned upside-down and rammed between the woman's legs all the way up through her body until the arms of Jesus appeared to be coming out of her crotch with one reaching forward and one reaching backward.

(Like a tail.)

Jesus's sad face emerging between the woman's legs, appearing as if the woman was birthing the Son of God. Dallas's mind latched onto something other than this gruesome sacrilege.

(Hovering?)

The impaled body floated several inches off the hardwood, dripping blood in unusual splatters that defied physics. Clearly, the woman, probably Maricela, had to be dead. An impulsive part of Dallas wanted to jump into the room and confront Vlad, but the rational part of her brain stopped her. Somehow viewing the scene through her phone provided an emotional detachment. It helped Dallas keep her shit together.

(Stop him how? And stop what? What am I seeing here?)

Dallas kept the video rolling.

Luca stretched and pointed his fingers like the evil Emperor in *Return of the Jedi* zapping Luke Skywalker with lightning. The crucifix spun until the dead Maricela faced her handsome husband. Her eyes had rolled back in her head. Luca raised his hands ever so slightly, and Maricela glided upward like a marionette on strings. Luca walked backward, and her body floated with him, following along.

Dancing. He held her in position with his left hand, looking like a manic magician. Then he raised his right hand toward the ceiling fan. The three swords bent toward him, curving like an upside-down blender bottom. Luca twirled his finger, and the blades spun faster and faster until they blurred invisible, even in the strobing light.

(Where's that light coming from, anyway?)

Luca took another step back, and like an orchestra conductor brought his hands together overhead. Maricela flew up into the spinning swords. Blood sprayed off the blades and splattered around the room. Maricela's head tumbled across the hardwood floor and landed under the coffin. Dropping his right hand, Luca stopped the ceiling fan. Blood poured off the blades. Stepping under, Luca tilted his head back, opened his mouth, and drank.

After drinking her blood, Luca held his hand a few inches apart as if grasping an invisible ball. His head nodded up and down like he was in a trance. After holding that position for a minute, with Maricela's decapitated body hovering in front of him, he pushed his hands away forcefully. The headless nude flew across the room and slammed into the wall so hard that the crucifix cut her from the inside-out. The whole house shook. The upside-down cross stayed mounted on the wall while Maricela's body opened up like a butterfly fillet and fell to the floor.

Splat.

Maricela's head stared at her inside-out body on the floor in front of her. Looking drained, Luca dropped his arms. The room went dark. Only vertical slats of ambient moonlight lit the room now. Taking his pipe with him, Luca climbed into his metal coffin. He laid down and closed the lid on himself. Her arms tired, Dallas stopped recording. She sat on the porch with her back against the wall and caught her breath. Strange how watching Luca butcher Maricela on the screen made the horror tolerable. The whole scene felt unreal, surreal, like watching a movie.

(Distant. This lack of anxiety. Disturbing.)

She poked her phone check that she got the footage. Only grainy sparkles and flashes of light played back. Her phone didn't capture anything except vague shadows. She tapped forward several minutes and discovered more shit footage. She tried after that. Also shit. She had nothing.

(Dammit.)

Dallas rotated through her enormous keyring until she found Maricela's house key. She considered the locked door.

(I must be crazy. I shouldn't go in there. I should walk away. I should call the cops.)

Dallas stood up and slid her key into the lock.

(No. No cops. Not for me.)

The door swung open with a creak and whine. She tiptoed inside and started a new video by panning the entire length of the room. She reviewed it.

(Still not enough light.)

Dallas considered the coffin and decided to take her chances. She opened the front door wide in case she would need to make a quick escape. Then she flicked on the light switch. The room lit. The ceiling fan swords twirled, still bent in their chopper formation. Dallas timed her duck like she was jumping double-dutch and kept her head down as she reached up and pulled the chain to stop the fan. The recently sharpened blades slowed and then stopped. Dallas got her first good look at the massacre.

Dallas immediately filmed the gruesome scene, and this time she had enough light. Panning the room from left to right, she started with the bloody, upside-down crucifix on the wall. She walked toward the cross and stopped when her toe bumped the mess on the floor. Dallas looked down through her phone. Mutilated tissue and organs could not be identified. While retracing the head's rolling path, Dallas followed a bloody trail. She zoomed on Maricela's face. The detached protection of the camera lost its magic.

Dallas gagged. Her heart raced. She couldn't breathe.

(I am crazy. What am I doing here?)

She gasped as she switched off the phone and shoved it into her pajama pocket. She felt a gentle tug on her arm and turned to face it. No one there. The coffin drew her fixator.

(Oh no, not the magnet.)

Dallas jerked her arm. But the strong magnetic attraction snapped her fixator against the side of the coffin.

Clang!

"Fuck."

Dallas cringed while still squatting next to the casket. Trapped by her arm, her heart raced even faster. And then the coffin lid opened. For the first time, she understood why snared animals gnawed off their paws to escape. She would have sawed off her limb to get away. She considered the crucifix and the ceiling mounted swords as options, but both were out of reach. Her mind freaked as the coffin opened further.

"You next," Luca said from inside.

With her arm still stuck, Dallas stood tall and leaned onto the lid. She forced it shut. Luca pushed back, and the coffin lid flapped up and down as they struggled for supremacy. Dallas rotated her arm and pulled on her fixator. It slid inch-by-inch up the side of the casket.

Scratch, screetch, scrape.

Metal-on-metal made a nails-on-the-chalkboard sound and left gnarly scratches in the shiny finish of the steel coffin. Dallas gave the lid a hard shove and then sat on top of it with her arm still stuck at her side. Somehow, the man who was just levitating a body around the room a few minutes ago couldn't push her weight.

"Where's all that bad guy strength now, motherfucker?" Dallas yelled at the coffin and beat on the lid with her free fist. As she sat, she focused on the open door and got her breathing under control. The sun rose in the east, casting a pink haze in the sky. A moment of clarity sunk in. Once she realized that all she had to do was walk away, her fixator snapped free from the coffin. She tapped it to the metal a few times, but it no longer stuck.

"Fickled magnet," she said.

(But I know. This lack of anxiety. That's why I'm free.)

Dallas sat on the lid for a while longer until it stopped popping up and down. Luca surrendered. Then she jumped off the coffin and dashed out the front door. She ran as fast as she could in flip-flops. Luca did not chase. Somehow, unarmed and in her pajamas, she had survived to fight him another day.

(Next time, I'll be ready. Next time, I'll take him down. I'm gonna stop the motherfucker.)

14

Sky Boss

After sleepwalking through the workday like a zombie, Dallas yawned at her locker. Todd popped his head around her locker door, startling her.

"Whatcha doin'?" he asked.

"God dammit, Todd." Dallas clutched her heart as she jumped back.

Clark and Steve appeared from around the corner after him.

"What's up with you, Mack?" Clark asked. "You've been off all day."

"I didn't get any sleep last night."

"Why not?" Clark asked, opening his locker next to hers.

"I was all amped up from—" Dallas closed her locker. "No. You wouldn't believe me."

"Oh, now this sounds juicy," Steve said, leaning in for the details.

Dallas threaded her padlock through the handle and squeezed it shut. It locked with a satisfying sound.

Click.

She shook her head. "It's too much."

"Now you have to tell us, Mack," Clark said, posting scrap paper notes on the inside of his locker with button magnets.

"You guys never met my neighbor," Dallas said. "But I told you about him. You know the guy I got all the bike parts from?"

"Right, the one that works at the junkyard," Clark said.

"This morning." Dallas paused and looked at her feet. "No. I can't say it."

"Come on, Mack. It's us," Todd said.

Dallas pulled out her iPhone, "How about I show you?"

"Works for me," Steve said.

Dallas cued up the video and pushed play. The *Three Amigos* huddled around the phone to watch the ninety-seven seconds of video footage.

"What is this?" Todd asked. "It's really dark and grainy."

"Shush!" Dallas said.

After zooming on Maricela's decapitated head, the video got all shaky.

"Whoa, you went Blair Witch on it," Steve said.

"So you're shooting horror movies now?" Clark asked.

"I knew you wouldn't believe me." Dallas shoved her phone in her pocket.

"Wait. Are you saying that was real?" Clark closed his locker.

"Yes, it happened this morning." Dallas walked away.

"No way." Todd followed after her.

"You gotta call the cops," Clark said.

Dallas stopped and spun to address Clark's suggestion, "Every time I go to Metro for help, I get fucked," Dallas said, unapologetically. "They're likely to say something like, 'how did you happen to be on the scene, Miss Mack?' And then

102

arrest my black ass again. I might not get out of jail next time."

"So this is really real?" Steve gestured toward the phone in her pocket. "Let me see that again."

Dallas handed him the phone. Steve and Todd rewatched the video.

"Well you can't go back there," Clark said, not needing to watch again.

"No kidding."

"But the police have to know. I mean, there's a dead body in that house," Clark said.

"Maybe they'll catch the guy," Todd said, without looking up from the video.

Dallas rolled her eyes, "Yeah, right."

"But this is evidence, right?" Todd asked.

"Well, last time I checked I'm still black," Dallas said showing him the back of her hand. Todd reached out to try and kiss it like a prince would kiss a lady's hand, and Dallas smacked his freckled paw away, "Really? Do you ever stop?"

The engineers walked to the time clock in a pack.

"Hey Mack, I could submit that video for you. You know, as an anonymous tip," Clark said.

"Yeah, like Crime Stoppers." Todd punched out.

"Hey guys, we could use Sky Boss." Steve punched out next.

"Sky Boss?" Dallas took her turn.

"Yeah. We fire up Sky Boss and send in the tip. Then watch the show," Clark said, punching his employee number into the clock.

"Will one of you please tell me what you're talking about?" Dallas led them toward the elevator.

"Sky Boss is the name of my quad copter. You know, my drone. I keep it in the back of my car," Steve said. "The only problem is that it only has a transmission radius of about a mile."

"Our trailer is one point two miles from your place," Todd said.

"Creepy that you know that, Todd. Real creepy," Dallas said. "We have to give it a shot."

They all got in the elevator and rode up together. Clark tapped away on his phone. "Hey Dallas, send me that video."

"Can I catch a ride with you all?" Dallas texted the file to Clark.

"You still don't have wheels?" Steve asked.

"Not yet. I'm going to buy something this weekend," Dallas said.

"Whatcha gonna get?" Steve asked.

"I don't know yet. Probably another Subaru. Best damn cars ever." Dallas tapped away at her phone as she walked and talked.

"How boring," Steve said.

"Well excuse me if I'm not up for the excitement of a Ford Fiesta Turbo," She laughed as the elevator doors opened and they exited into the lobby as a glob.

"What's that dude's name next door?" Clark asked.

"Luca Bogdan," Dallas said.

"How do you spell Bogdan?" Clark asked.

"B-O-G-D-A-N."

"B-O-D–" Clark said.

"No. B-O-G– You know what, gimme that, I'll enter the data myself," Dallas said as they crossed over the top of the damn into the employee parking lot. They piled into Steve's little orange car. Clark acquiesced the front seat to

Dallas without her asking. She entered all the information about what she witnessed that morning. She and Clark passed the phone back and forth. It only took them about five minutes to complete the web-form.

Todd hung over the seat and dug around in the hatchback until he emerged with Sky Boss.

Steve scolded him in the rearview mirror, "You know you're not supposed to touch that."

Todd spun one of the propellers with his finger.

Clark scrolled through his phone. "I'm ready to submit this anonymous tip."

"Go for it," Dallas said.

Clark made a grand hand gesture of fancy pointing and pressed the submit button on his phone screen. "And it is done."

They chattered like excited high school kids after the last bell on a Friday afternoon the whole way to the trailer of the *Three Amigos*. Even though she'd had no sleep, Dallas felt energized.

(I might even be having fun.)

Time flew, and when Dallas looked up, Steve pulled into his driveway. They parked. Todd hopped out of the car and held the drone in the air like a boy playing with a toy plane. He made engine noises as he ran in a figure-eight in the driveway.

"Vroom, vroom!"

Steve pulled a yellow pelican case from the hatchback and marched toward the trailer. Using the wooden steps as a workbench, he turned to yell back at Todd, "Do not drop that. That's a thousand-dollar piece of technology. It's not a toy."

Todd gave Steve the thumbs up.

Steve sighed and addressed Dallas, "I'm going to get set up here."

"Good. Let's get this bird in the air," Dallas said.

Steve opened his case and spread his gear all over the porch. He snatched the quadcopter from Todd, and gently set it next to the remote control. Steve mounted his iPhone onto the remote console and connected it via wifi. When he powered up the drone, his phone screen display synced. Steve fiddled with one of the RC joysticks, and the mounted camera tilted and panned. When she wasn't looking, he zoomed on Dallas's thong sticking out the top of her skinny jeans. The huddled *Three Amigos* snickered like middle-schoolers at a loud fart. Dallas shot them a look, and Steve covered the phone screen so she couldn't see.

"We're ready to fly. Dallas. Enter your street address here." Steve pointed at the screen.

"I can do it," Todd volunteered.

"Don't even," Dallas said.

"Sky Boss will follow the GPS coordinates to your house. We can fly in manually from there."

Dallas awkwardly tapped her information into Steve's phone while he watched over her shoulder. Then she handed the unit to him, and he pressed a few buttons.

"Everyone stand back. Sky Boss ready for lift off," Steve announced as he pressed the power button.

The four horizontal propellers whirled, and everyone took two steps back in unison.

Whurrrlllzzzzzzzzz.

"My goodness that's loud," Dallas said.

Steve pushed one of the joysticks, and the drone hovered off the porch. It climbed higher and higher. The crew all stared up at it, but Steve looked at his phone. He tilted the camera downward and took video of everyone.

"Wave for the camera," Steve said.

Everyone smiled and waved. Steve started recording. He tapped a command on his phone and switched into automatic navigation mode, and the drone took off, heading northwest.

Whurrrlllzzzzzzzzz.

The whirling buzz got higher in pitch and volume as the drone accelerated. Then the sound faded as the quadcopter shrank and disappeared from view behind a cluster of tall pinion pines. The gang gathered around Steve to catch the drone's-eye-view of the neighborhood. Steve maneuvered the camera to capture a panorama of the Las Vegas Valley horizon. Then he panned downward and followed the traffic on Boulder Highway for a while. In a few minutes, the drone dropped altitude and slowed down.

"Hey, that's my development," Dallas said, recognizing the gated entrance and the small dog park in the center of her master planned community.

The drone zoomed on her street, and she recognized the leafless trees and roofline of her house. She'd viewed it on Google Earth a hundred times. Steve zoomed on the backyard, and Bella's freshly dug grave filled the screen. Maneuvering the joysticks and pressing a button, Steve switched into manual mode. And the drone jerked around while hovering in the backyard.

"May I?" Dallas asked reaching for the controls.

Steve reluctantly handed them over. Then he leaned in and gave her a brief introduction to flying RC drones. "This one on the left controls the throttle. And this one on the right controls the direction."

"Like a Playstation controller," Todd said.

"It is not a game," Steve snipped, insulted. He pointed at a red button. "Push this button here, to switch to the camera controls. Then left is tilt and right is pan. Got it?"

Dallas nodded as she oversteered, and the drone jerked around.

"Easy does it. It's sensitive."

Pleased with the fine dexterity of her rehabilitating injury, Dallas gently pushed the controls. She got the feel for flying quickly. After taking a small lap around her backyard with the drone, she dashed off to the dog park and harassed a jogger. Then, she flew back to her house and zoomed in on Bella's grave. "Okay, I think I've got it."

"Why don't you take it up and get a better view of what's going on around your house," Clark suggested.

Steve pointed to the control for altitude and Dallas nodded. She flew upward and watched her house shrink on the screen. In a few seconds, she saw cop cars clogging up her cul-de-sac.

(Like the morning they found Ramone.)

Metro officers shrunk into little avatars as Dallas flew higher and higher.

"Okay, okay. That's far enough," Steve said.

Dallas released the control, and the drone hovered in space. She pressed the red button and moved the camera around until it focused on Marcela's house. They watched police march in and out her front door like busy soldier ants. Two more police cars rolled up with their lights and sirens on.

"The front door must still be open. I don't see Luca anywhere," Dallas said, panning and zooming while squinting at the phone screen. "This is great and all, but I can't see what's going on inside the house."

"Well yeah, I mean we are flying outside," Steve said.

Out of patience, Dallas jammed the joystick and the drone dove downward toward the front of her neighbor's house.

"Whoa, whoa, what are you doing? Slow down. Slow down!" Steve yelled.

Dallas flew the drone straight in the front door and released the throttle inside the dining room. She pressed the red button and panned around the room. Maricela's body was gone. Her head was gone. The coffin gone. Blood splatter, the sword-ceiling fan, and the gory upside-down crucifix on the wall remained. Dallas zoomed on the fan blades.

"Look at this," she said. "They're sharp. Spinning swords."

Steve and Clark stared at the screen.

"You're recording this, right?" Clark asked.

"Of course," Steve said.

Dallas panned the camera. "That's where I found his coffin."

A big, marine-looking cop's face filled the screen. They all jumped back.

"Shit!" Dallas said as the cop grabbed for the drone. Rather than back away, she pushed the throttle and the drone lurched forward, bashing the cop in the face. "It's that prick, McCoy."

Smack.

"Ooof," the cop whelped as the drone whacked him above his right eyebrow then bounced off. He grasped at the drone like King Kong swat-grabbing at biplanes while hanging on the Empire State building.

Steve got nervous. "Get out of there. *Oh my God!* Give me the controls. Give me. Gimme!" He jumped up and down.

Dallas yanked her stick and pushed the off camera button at the same time. Swerving her hands and leaning her whole body in the direction she wanted the drone to go, she pointed it toward the front door. Then she flew out of the house. She buzzed another cop on the way out. McCoy chased after the drone, but once she got outside, Dallas increased altitude. It flew straight up.

"Up, up up!" She said, encouraging it.

"Yes! Hurry, get away," Steve said, over her shoulder.

"I need some popcorn. Great show," Clark gaffed.

The drone climbed higher and higher. Both Dallas and Steve relaxed once it reached several dozen feet over Maricela's Spanish tile roof. Frustrated Metro officers huddled and looked up at the drone. They discussed. They pointed. They strategized. Dallas and Steve laughed. She zoomed on McCoy's angry face. But then he reached for his side arm, unholstered it, drew his pistol and fired a single shot. He hit. The drone sputtered and cracked then fell to the ground and shattered. Steve watched in amazement as Sky Boss fell.

"Damn!" Clark said, "Sky Boss down."

"Fuck you, Clark," Steve said.

Dallas handed the controller back to Steve. "Sorry." She shoved her hands in her jean pockets.

Steve's shoulders slumped as he took the controller. He watched a big black tactical boot stomp through the lens of his webcam. The feed went to static. He looked like he might cry.

"We're gonna need a bigger Boss," Clark said.

"Luca's gone. We have to find him," Dallas said. "I bet he packed up his coffin, took Maricela's remains, and skipped out of there."

"Who is this guy, anyway?" Steve asked.

"He's a killer. He killed my dog. Then he killed my dog-walker, Ramone. Then he killed my neighbor, Maricela."

"Okay, I get it. He killed your dog, but why not let Metro handle it," Clark asked.

"Because I'm next," Dallas said in a flat tone.

"How do you know that?" Clark asked.

"He told me so," Dallas said. "Look, I understand if you guys want out. But I have to stop him. I have no choice."

"I'm in," Todd exclaimed.

"Well, this shit's starting to get good. I gotta see where the story goes," Clark said as he stood on the other side of Dallas and put his arm around her. The three stood together and stared at Steve.

"Well fuck me," Steve said, defeated. He tossed his useless remote controller onto the porch. "Guess we're some sort of team."

15

Lackluster Muster

Saturday morning, no one could tell that a slaughter happened on that cozy little cul-de-sac the morning before. If she hadn't shot video, Dallas wouldn't have believed it herself. She took a lap around her house while waiting for the crew to arrive.

(Should we give ourselves a name? The crew. The team. The gang. The Four Amigos. Maybe just The Amigos.)

Last night, after Sky Boss got shot down by Metro, they decided to gather at her place. Their assignment: get a good night's sleep and then pick their best fighting gear and weaponry and bring it back to her house. They needed to take a collective inventory.

Dallas had not a single weapon in her whole house. After living in Vegas nearly her entire adult life, she should have picked up a gun or two by now. Everyone in Vegas had at least one gun.

(But not me. I'm terrified of guns.)

She looked around in the kitchen. A few dull butcher knives. She bought them and never sharpened them.

(Who bothers? I'm no cook.)

She looked around in the living room, then the dining room. Nothing. Then she dug around in the garage. Her home workshop housed all kinds of tools.

(Hand and power.)

"Every tool is a weapon if you hold it right," she said, encouraging herself as she remembered her father. Except, she'd fought Luca once and saw what he did to Maricela. She picked a ratchet handle from the set.

(This probably won't be enough to take him down.)

She focused on her cherished welding gear. Among a vast collection of sparkers, hammers, torches, and masks, sat her brand new Tomahawk handheld electric plasma cutter. Now that was something. That had potential. She picked up the torch and admired it, then her doorbell rang. Dallas hustled to the door, peeked through the peephole and saw Todd standing with a backpack slung over his shoulder. She swung the door open to greet her friends, "Hey, guys."

Steve had parked on the street. He climbed halfway into the back of his hatchback and kept digging. She spotted Clark in a full suit of shiny medieval armor, stiffly clanking up her driveway. His long red velvet cape flapped behind him. His face shield was flipped up, so she saw his smile. Dallas couldn't help herself. She laughed instantly.

"What is this supposed to be?" Dallas giggled, then laughed so hard that she could barely speak.

Todd chuckled, "It's his 'suit.'"

"The only suit I own, I'm proud to say," Clark announced as he stepped onto her porch. He made a fist and knocked on his chest.

Clang, clang.

"I'm ready for battle."

"You look like the Tin Man from the *Wizard of Oz.*" Dallas laughed and laughed until she hyperventilated. She couldn't stop, even then. Her belly ached from laughing so hard.

She invited Todd and Clark inside. Then came Steve, dressed head to toe in digital desert camouflage. She hustled to the front door carrying two heavy gun cases. He even had poof-dirt colored tactical boots.

(Light beige.)

"I've got more," Steve said, setting the cases inside the door, then dashing back down the driveway for the others. On his third trip from the car, Steve let out a battle cry, "Bring on the apocalypse!"

Following behind, Todd carried two more gun cases inside and shut the door behind them. They gathered in the kitchen.

"How come there are never any women around?" Steve sat his smallest case on the center island.

"Excuse me? I'm a woman," Dallas said.

"You don't count. Don't you have any girlfriends?" Steve asked.

"Girlfriends?" Dallas made a tread-lightly face.

"I mean girls that are friends." Steve opened his case.

"I've always been a tomboy."

"What about black friends?" Todd asked.

(Goddamn it, Todd.)

Dallas just stared with her mouth hanging open. She had no words.

"I think he means, where's your family?" Clark asked, trying to defuse the tension.

(Jesus. Getting grilled here.)

"Where's yours, Clark?"

Clark paused, stunned and hurt. He pointed at the guys. "This is it. These guys are my family. We've been together since college."

"Let's talk about guns instead." Uncomfortable, Steve pulled out a semi-automatic Desert Eagle. "This one's a forty-four magnum."

Dallas ducked below the counter when she saw the hand cannon. "Whoa, put that thing away."

"It's not loaded," Steve said.

"I don't care. I don't want it out. Not in my house."

Steve sighed and put the pistol back in its case. "Fine. You're the one who said, 'bring your best gear and weapons.'"

"That's true. You did," Clark said. "And I'm your white knight in shining armor, Mack."

"Quite literally." With the gun away, Dallas stood tall and giggled at the sight of him. "I'm sorry, I can't look at you without laughing."

"Laugh it up, Mack. You'll see," Clark said as he lowered his face shield and turned toward Todd. In his best Joker impression, Clark quoted dialogue from *The Dark Knight*. "Come on. Come on. I want you to do it. Come on. Hit me. Hit me!"

"No way," Todd said. "I'll bust my knuckles."

Clark raised his face shield and said matter-a-factly, "My point exactly."

"Sure, Clark, whatever you say," Dallas said. "Hey, Todd, what's in your pack?"

"Oh, here. I'll show you." Todd unzipped his bag. He pulled out an X-Men comic book, volume two, issue one. It had a muscly red guy on the cover wearing a purple cape.

Dallas took the comic book. "God dammit, Todd."

"No, this is good shit," Todd said. "You can be like Magneto."

"Can we please talk about something else?" Dallas insisted as she tossed the comic on the counter.

"Okay," Clark said, clanking across the kitchen. "Let's talk about your gear and weapons. We all brought ours for show-and-tell. What have you got?"

"Not much I'm afraid." Dallas paced.

"Seriously, you must have some sort of weapon around," Steve said. "A little lady pistol?"

"Nope. Clark's got a point. I've got nothing." She took two round lime-shaped refrigerator magnets and stuck them on the torso of Clark's armor, right where his nipples should have been.

"Ha, ha. Very funny, Mack." Clark twisted the magnets. He couldn't resist playing with them.

"What if someone broke in? You're always alone here in this house," Steve asked.

"She's not alone right now," Clark said.

"I could always mock a burglar to death. I've got a lot of snarky comments."

"Nah, huh-uh. I'm raiding your closet. There's got to be something," Steve said, handing the comic book back to Todd as he marched up the stairs.

The crew followed him into the master bedroom. Dallas trailed behind them all. By the time she caught up, Steve and Todd had already invaded in her walk-in closet.

"Whoa," Todd said, eyeing an extensive collection of leather fetish-ware.

"Yeah, guys, there's nothing in there," Dallas said from behind, pushing her way past and into her closet.

As if he were shopping in a high-end boutique, Steve went through the rack hanger-by-hanger. "Corset, corset,

corset," he mumbled. "Not very practical for combat. Oh wait, here we go, black leather vest." He pulled it off the hanger and tossed it at her. "You can get that over your mechanical mess of an arm, right?"

Embarrassed, Dallas nodded without making eye contact.

"Yeah. Okay, now for bottoms." Steve went further down the rack. "Mini skirt, mini skirt, mini skirt… I sense a theme here. Silver sure has his preferences."

(How'd he know about Sil?)

"Shut up!" Dallas rolled her eyes.

Clark lifted his face shield. "Don't mind us."

"We all know you've been banging the boss," Steve said.

"What? How? I mean… No, I'm not."

"Everybody at the dam knows," Todd said.

"And nobody cares," Clark added.

"Well, shit," Dallas said, defeated.

"Ah, here we go, black leather pants," Steve said, pulling them off a trouser hanger. He tossed the pants at her. "Now shoes." Steve turned to a stack of sawed-off, foot-wide sections of PVC pipe that Dallas bolted together into a shoe rack. He pulled out shoes pair-by-pair. "Heels." He tossed them aside. "Stiletto heels, clunky heels, stripper heels, stupid heels, and more heels. Aren't you tall enough already? Why do you need all these heels?"

"He likes them," Dallas said, embarrassed.

"What do *you* like?" Steve asked.

Dallas pulled out a pair of black knee-high, lace-up, steel toe boots with lug soles. "Not heels."

"All right guys. Let's get out," Steve said. "Give the woman some privacy." He herded the men out of the closet. "Now, get dressed," he said as he closed the door behind them.

The *Three Amigos* waited for Dallas in her bedroom. Todd bounced on the bed, while the two stood around pretending not to look at anything.

"Exactly how'd you fit in the Fiesta?" Steve asked while eyeing Clark's armor.

"You were there," Clark said.

"I saw that you did it. But how?"

"Obviously I did. I didn't teleport here."

"I better not find scratches on the Fiesta interior."

"Whoa," Todd said as he opened the nightstand drawer and discovered a magnificent collection of sex toys. He gathered up an armful of dildos, vibrators, leather straps, rings, and other things he'd never saw before and tossed them on the bedspread.

Dallas came out of the bedroom in time to catch the invasive action. "God dammit, Todd."

"Bam! Look at you," Clark said.

"Now there's a kick-ass outfit," Steve said.

Dallas pulled the zipper on her vest higher, and her cleavage squeezed together. "Can't I just wear jeans?"

"You mean like Todd here?" Steve asked.

"Pfft. Good point. Leather it is," Dallas said.

"Besides, leather is a kind of protective armor. It's not as good as, well, my armor, but it's something."

Dallas pointed at her marital aids on the bed. "Let's address this." She crossed the room, opened her top dresser drawer, pulled it out all the way and dumped the contents onto the bed. Even more sex toys tumbled out of the drawer; clamps, pumps, slings, handcuffs, whips, paddles, and cat-o-nine tails.

"Everything kinky you could imagine and more," Steve said with wide eyes.

"All gifts."

"For you or for him?" Clark asked.

Steve picked up a fancy ping-pong paddle and whacked Clark's armor. It echoed.

Clang, -ang, -ang, -ang.

Clark picked out the whip and cuffs. "These could be useful. Bring them."

Dallas rolled up the bullwhip and hooked it to her belt and shoved the cuffs in her back pocket.

"Maybe there's a weapon here," Todd said waving a big, floppy, neon-green, studded, alien dildo in the air like a dagger.

Dallas shuffled through her inventory, tossing things aside. "Useless, broken, useless." She considered a firm, giant, black dildo in a harness, the kind that was meant to be worn by a woman and used on, well usually, another woman. "Uh, I can't even…" She tossed it aside.

Steve pulled out a ball gag. "We can always go all Pulp Fiction on this guy. I've got a shotgun downstairs." He gestured to the strap-on. "and that contraption… So all we need is a samurai sword."

"She's gonna get medieval on your ass," Clark said.

And they all busted out laughing hysterically. And after they caught their breath, Dallas spoke up.

"Can I tell you something guys?" She asked shyly.

"Sure," Steve said.

"I used to call you all *The Three Amigos*," Dallas said, stacking up the sex toys in a pile.

"What?" Steve asked.

"Back before I knew you, I used to make fun of you guys and call you *The Three Amigos*," Dallas said, as she sat on the edge of the bed.

There the men stood, Clark in his suit of armor and red cape, Steve looking like a crazy doomsday prepper, and Todd holding an alien cock like a floppy dagger.

"I don't get it," Todd said.

"Clark, Steve, Todd. You know," Dallas pointed at Clark. "Chevy Chase." Then she pointed at Steve, "Steve Martin." And lastly, she pointed at Todd. "Martin Short?"

"Martin?" Todd mumbled, confused.

(Still clueless.)

They looked at each other and shook their heads.

"Never mind. Anyway, I thought it was funny to mock you. And I'm sorry I made fun of you guys."

"Okay." Steve shrugged.

"Now that we're like a gang, we ought to have a name," Dallas said.

"But now there's four of us," Todd said.

"Like *The Four Amigos?*" Steve asked.

"How, about just *The Amigos?*" Dallas suggested.

They all nodded.

"I like that," Clark said.

"Enough of this talky talk. Let's go shoot some shit in the desert," Steve said. "We'll need more targets."

Todd made a naughty boy face and wiggled the alien cock.

"Excellent," Steve said. "Let's go out and shoot some plastic penises."

16

∩

Hubcap Graveyard

The Amigos crammed into Steve's tangerine Ford with their gear. Dallas and Todd conceded shotgun to Clark because neither wanted to be squished next to his armor in the backseat.

(If he'd even fit.)

Dallas squeezed behind the driver's seat. Before getting in, Clark slid the front passenger seat backward as far as it could go, jamming Todd's shins.

Uncomfortable and impatient, they waited for Clark to wedge his shiny metal ass into the front seat. Clark tried going in head first, but that didn't work. So ass first, he fell into the seat. Somehow, he managed to get his limbs inside. He closed the door. As soon as Steve heard the door latch, he drove down the street. Speeding, they reached the edge of town in less than ten minutes.

"I gotta get my own wheels," Dallas said.

"Yeah. Why haven't you done that yet?" Steve asked, looking in the rearview.

"Because I've been spending all my spare time running around with your crazy asses," Dallas said. "I haven't had a chance."

"Sounds like it needs to become a priority," Steve said.

"True." Dallas nodded. "Tomorrow. Sunday. No matter what. Tomorrow, I buy a new car."

"Whatcha gonna get?" Todd asked.

"Something big," Dallas said, fidgeting to get semi-comfortable. "With lots of leg room." Her knee bumped against Todd's. "Hey, Steve, where are we going, anyway?"

"*The Hubcap Graveyard*," he answered into his rearview mirror.

"Why's it called *The Hubcap—*" She saw the answer.

Where the bumpy road came to a T-intersection, rows and rows of hubcaps lodged into the desert dirt, like small round rusty tombstones. They formed a three-dimensional arrow that pointed the way.

"We follow the hubcaps," Clark said from inside his rattling suit of armor.

"Do they even make hubcaps anymore?" Dallas asked.

"Not really. Everyone's got rims now. But all those old hubcaps had to go somewhere," Steve said.

"It started in the 50's, back before Henderson was even an official city. People came out here to shoot in the desert. Regulars would leave a hubcap behind as a tribute. Others copied. You know, monkey see, monkey do. And now it's all this," Clark said, gesturing out the window at thousands of hubcaps glistening in the desert sun.

"This used to be a decent drive into the desert. But the city grew into the foothills," Steve said.

"So, why does it smell like bananas in here?" Dallas changed the topic.

"Oh, that's the fruit," Steve said.

"Fruit?" Dallas asked.

"Oh, yeah. Overripe fruit makes the best shooting targets," Steve said.

"We don't shoot flimsy paper bullseyes like everyone else," Todd said.

"No way, Mr. Top Shot here likes to keep things interesting," Clark said.

"And we're here," Steve announced as he pulled into an unmarked parking area.

Todd helped Clark out of the car. Then, without conversation or instruction, The Amigos worked as a team to unload. Like fire ants on a trail, they followed Steve from the hatchback to the edge of the pit, down the fifty percent grade of the embankment, to the destination, and back again.

"What is this place?" Dallas asked, looking at least a half mile across the bottom of the pit before the embankment rose on the other side.

"Rainwater runoff reservoir," Steve said pointing at the gravel wall on the far side of the pit. "And that makes for the perfect bullet-stopping berm."

"Is this legal?" Dallas asked.

"It sure is," Steve said. "God bless Ameri-fucking-ca!"

"We're outside Metro lines. Places like this have been mapped out for shooting all around Vegas," Clark added.

The men worked together to set up targets, while Dallas kicked broken plates and shotgun shells left by shooters of the past in the rocky dirt. When finished, four over-tall wooden sawhorses stood in a row. Todd and Steve fetched various targets from a laundry basket, tied string around each of them, and hung them from the center two-by-four of each.

"Okay, line up," Steve said.

Dallas stood in front of the floppy green alien dildo. She loved the texture of that thing but never understood why anyone would manufacture a flaccid sex toy. She looked forward to killing that green silicon cock. It swayed while hanging by its trio of weirdly shaped balls at the end of a string. Clark chose to shoot at a silver vibrator.

"For an added challenge." He twisted the end and turned it on. It buzzed and bobbled on its tether. Then Clark returned to his place behind the firing line.

Todd took his place in front of a teddy bear holding a heart. He had tied a noose around its neck and watched it swing like a convicted bank robber of olden western times. And Steve would shoot at a hanging, bruised banana with a bow tied around its stem.

"I love shooting fruit. Its the most realistic target I've found," Steve said. He patted the grip of his Desert Eagle . 44 Magnum, resting in the holster on his gun belt. Then he sat one case in front of each of his friends. "You may open your case, but do not handle your guns yet." Steve drew a long line in front of them by dragging the heal of his boot through the dirt. "Nobody crosses this line," he said sternly, pointing at it.

Everyone followed his instructions. After a brief safety speech, Steve gave some basic firearms instruction, reviewing loading, stance, grip, aiming and trigger pull. Steve demonstrated each technique with his impressive pistol. Then he told everyone they could hold their guns. Clark and Todd had been through all this before but not wanting to pressure Dallas, respectfully waited through Steve's lecture. Dallas had to shoot with her left, and she sucked at doing things with her left hand. She would have her fixator for at least another month.

(No way I can fire a gun with my busted side.)

Clark uncased a 9mm Glock and slid the loaded magazine into place. Careful with his chainmail gloves, he could barely grip his firearm. Todd pulled out a Ruger .22

124

revolver and loaded it with his tiny ammo. Dallas embraced her long-barreled Smith and Wesson .357 magnum revolver with fear. It felt heavy, and she still thought it looked like an exaggerated cartoon toy.

"This looks like Dirty Harry's gun. Why did you give me one so big?" Dallas asked.

"Dirty Harry carries a six-shot, double action, .44 Magnum Smith & Wesson revolver. What you're holding there is only a .357 Magnum," Steve corrected her.

"More information than I needed, Steve."

Steve made an indignant face. "All right then. Everyone in position?" Steve asked, stepping behind the line and taking aim at his target.

"Roger."

"Uh, huh."

"Yeah."

"Great. Ready. Aim… Fire!"

All four guns stagger-fired. A mess.

Dallas flinched. Her pistol kicked and bit her hand so hard that she dropped it in the dirt. "Fucker," she spat and didn't bother to pick up her gun. Instead, she massaged the swelling web between her thumb and forefinger with her splinted hand.

Three of the four targets remained unscathed. Everyone missed except Steve, who blew away the bottom half of his banana target. Peal bits and banana guts splattered the desert dust. The stem still hung from its bow. It rocked violently on the end of its string, spinning and rotating to show all its awesome, fruity carnage.

Clark fumbled with his Glock. He couldn't even get his steel-clad finger all the way through the trigger guard. "How'd you even fire your weapon," Steve asked once he saw Clark's problem. Steve brought him a twelve-gauge, pump-action, Winchester shotgun. Everyone watched as Clark aimed and fired at the hanging vibrator. This time, he hit. The plastic splintered, spilling shattered electronics and battery acid into the sand. The butt of the shotgun banged against his shoulder and left a significant dent in his armor.

Clang, thump.

Clark rubbed his metal shoulder with his clunky gloved hand and felt nothing. Steve dashed to the laundry basket and retrieved a red heart pillow with the word "Love" embroidered in white. He popped the pink rubber ball out of the fetish gag and dashed back to Clark with the leather strap. Steve placed the heart over the dent in Clark's shoulder and buckled the leather gag around his armpit.

"Aw. Now the Tin Man has a heart," Dallas said.

"Don't mind her," Steve said. "Take another shot, Clark."

"But it's swinging really fast."

"What great practice!" Steve pumped his fist in the air, "Now shoot it!"

Clark pumped the shotgun, and the spent shell popped out. He aimed and fired. He hit again, completely obliterating what remained of the broken vibrator.

"Yes!" Clark yelled triumphantly.

"How was that recoil?" Steve asked.

"Much better."

"Everyone hold your fire," Steve said. He checked to make sure all fingers were off all triggers and then went to check Todd's target. "You did good, buddy."

"I did? I thought I missed."

"Nah. You shot its eye out," Steve said, cutting the noose with his field knife. He brought the stuffed bear back to Todd. A dark hole replaced the black button eye, and a small plume of white stuffing blew out the back of the teddy bear's head.

"I hate guns," Dallas said, still rubbing her hand. "This isn't working for me."

"Fine, then whip out your whip. Give that a shot," Steve said.

"What?" Dallas looked confused.

"You heard me. Strike that alien cock with your whip. A target is a target, regardless of the weapon," Steve said.

Unsure, Dallas stepped up to the line. She pulled her whip off her belt and held the handle in her left, letting the end fall and uncoil at her feet. Steve adjusted her stance. Then he stepped far off to her side.

(Everyone's staring at me.)

Dallas had always suffered from performance anxiety. Even as a great runner with a perfect stride, she never won a race in her life. She did better with cross country but always blew it at the finish line. The sun hung low in the sky behind them, casting a long shadow ahead of her. The sight of her tall, sexy, whip-wielding silhouette made her feel embarrassed and self-conscious.

(I'm going to choke.)

She thought of Indiana Jones and raised her left hand high above her head. Then she snapped her wrist downward as if using a hammer. The tail-end of the whip snapped up and hit her in the cheek, then got tangled in her fixator on her other arm. Dallas felt the sting instantly. Then a warm, sticky pool of blood worked its way to the surface and trickled down her face. Before Dallas had a chance to process her feelings, Clark came to her rescue. Her friend took the bullwhip, coiled it up and tossed it aside. Then he wiped the dripping blood away with his chain-mailed hand. Red smeared across steel links.

"We're going to have to find you another weapon," Clark said with kind, soft words.

A whirlwind of feelings rushed around in her head and heart as tears flooded her eyes. Fresh blood filled the cut on her cheek, "Clark?"

Clark wiped away her teardrop. "I'm sure that stung. That would bring tears to my eyes too."

The sun began to set on their long day. Fatigue and failure replaced *The Amigos'* morning enthusiasm. Their impressive inventory of firearms meant little when no one, except for Steve, had the confidence and skills to wield them effectively. They stood defeated before they ever discussed the enemy or strategy. The guys might have seen the video, but only Dallas truly understood the magnitude of the evil they faced. It felt comforting to be with friends, but deep down, Dallas knew.

(We don't stand a chance against Luca.)

"All right, let's tear it down," Steve said gesturing to the targets.

As they disassembled the saw horses, headlights blared down on them from above. Everyone turned to discover they were not alone.

17

Battle Pit

An oversized rusty pickup truck plunged down the embankment and barreled toward the shooting line. Its giant knubby tires spun, kicking rocks and dust everywhere. Gravity pulled the truck into a slide on the steep incline. Within seconds, the truck hit the bottom of the pit, bounced on all fours and skidded directly for Dallas. She dove to the side in time to avoid being hit. The pickup came to a rocking stop. Its idling engine rumbled.

Stunned and blinded by headlights, Steve got to his feet and smacked the dust from his camouflaged pants. "Drunk locals."

Luca climbed down the side-step of the lifted truck. His pipe-smoke lingered and mixed with the stifling dust cloud. He clenched his teeth on the pipe stem. He inhaled smoke. He exhaled smoke. And with his tongue mostly missing, he should have had trouble speaking. Dallas shivered when Luca called her name, "Dallas."

(Crystal clear. Fucking crystal clear.)

Still, on the ground and in shock, Dallas trembled. Before she had a chance to run, Luca took four steps and swooped in to grab a fistful of her hair. Violently, he hoisted her. Her hair broke off in his fist as she scrambled to her feet. A slave to momentum, Dallas reeled toward the bed of his idling monster truck. She ducked for cover, and her fixator stuck to the tailgate. Yanking, she could not break free of the magnetic force. Dallas panicked.

(What the hell with this thing?)

Clark aimed his shotgun. Before he could fire, Luca waved two hands toward him in a pushing motion. Clark's feet swept off the ground, and he flew backward, landing forty feet down range. Without the proper grip, the impact of his landing bumped his finger against the trigger. Buckshot blasted straight up into the night sky. The butt of the shotgun hit Clark in the head where his open face shield left him vulnerable. The recoil broke his nose and knocked him cold. The gun dropped to his side. Clark fell limp.

"Dallas," Luca said in his vampire accent.

She yelled from behind the truck, "Fuck you, Luca!"

"Not Luca." He sauntered toward her. "Am Vlad. Your God."

A shot ricocheted off the open door of the truck and missed Vlad. More annoyed than frightened, he turned toward the shooter. Steve aimed his Desert Eagle at him, trying not to shake with anticipation. He'd never actually fired at a real person before. The two stared each other down. Dallas crawled under the back of the truck for cover, twisting her stuck arm behind her. Her fixator scraped and inched along the tail bumper.

"I'll shoot," Steve warned.

"You did," Vlad looked at the bullet hole in his truck then back at Steve. "And missed." Vlad smiled and strolled toward him.

"Get down on the ground," Steve yelled, gesturing with his gun.

Vlad continued to walk staring him down the entire time.

"I mean it. I'll shoot," Steve said.

Vlad held his hands up in a posed that mocked police surrender and kept walking. Steve panicked and fired. Once he pulled the trigger, he did it again and again and again. He kept shooting until he emptied his eight-round magazine. Vlad held out his hands as if ordering traffic to halt and the bullets slowed and slowed until they froze. The slugs hung in the air. Then Vlad made a baseball-tossing gesture, and all the bullets flew back toward Steve. He raised his arm to protect his face as the bullets pelted him like angry hale and fell. Steve looked like he wanted to cry, but he stood transfixed in disbelief.

"Whoa, that's some *Matrix-like* shit right there," Todd said unintentionally drawing Vlad's attention.

"God Dammit, Todd," Dallas whispered, still struggling to free her fixator from the truck.

Vlad raised his hands skyward, like a Viking summoning a Norse God. The sound of rocks scraping metal echoed in the distance.

(From everywhere.)

Thwing, Twing, Ting, -ing, -ing.

A flock of spinning hover-discs flew overhead like mini UFOs. One-by-one, Vlad pelted Todd with the summoned hubcaps. The first landed as body shots. Todd bounced around like a rag doll. Then Vlad delivered a couple of nasty spinners to his head. Todd collapsed as hubcaps bombarded him from every direction. In no time, they buried him. Vlad kept hammering away, but Todd hid safely inside his metal cocoon.

(Impromptu armor.)

Watching Todd get beat made Dallas rage inside. Anxiety waned. Adrenalin still flowed, but suddenly her fixator broke free, releasing her arm. Dallas scrambled from under the truck and crouched in a squat to stay hidden. She ducked while scooting alongside the vehicle. Then she climbed behind the wheel. Vlad didn't see her move, but Steve did.

Moving stealthily, Steve pulled his spare magazine from his gun-belt. He swapped it with the empty and cocked the slide of his gun. He looked up at Dallas and nodded. The headlights kept him from seeing into the cab of the truck. Even with night sights, targeting got harder now that the sun had set. Vlad attacked Todd in the dark, and Steve hadn't practiced night shooting before. So, he moved closer.

Dallas lifted the handle and closed the truck door without making noise.

(Automatic. Lucky. I can't shift with his hand.)

With her fixator, her wrist wouldn't move in a stick shift direction, but she could pull the steering column shifter. Dallas rolled down the window and waved her good arm at Steve. She pressed the brake and shifted the truck into drive. She remembered her bleeding cheek and checked herself in the rearview. The blood had dried into a crust. Being behind the wheel of a monster truck gave her a surge of confidence. With both hands on the wheel, she waited for her cue from Steve.

Steve moved as close as he could without blocking her path. He stopped and aimed. He waited for Vlad to rest between hubcap assaults and then pulled the trigger. The first shot missed high and right. Vlad stopped attacking Todd and threw a threatening glare at Steve. He shot again, and this time grazed the side of Vlad's face. The bullet shot off the lower part of his earlobe. Blood splurted everywhere. Vlad marched toward Steve, who fired off three more shots, missing everyone.

(Go!)

Dallas slammed the gas pedal to the floor, and all four wheels spun in the dirt. When the treads caught, she lurched forward. Without much distance to generate speed, she rammed into Vlad. His body snagged the undercarriage. Dallas accelerated, dragging him along the bottom of the pit. Racing with him under her, she ran out of space near the end of the reservoir. She slammed the brake, yanked the wheel to the left, and spun out into a satisfying dust-spitting donut.

She flashed her headlights twice to *The Amigos* on the other side. Then Vlad appeared, hanging off the side of her door. He reached through the open window and grabbed her throat, choking her. Acting on instinct, she struck him in the eyes with a v-neck strike using her fixator arm. The splint knocked him so hard that he fell off the truck. She blinded him long enough to make another move.

(Go. Go!)

Dallas stomped the accelerator and sped back for her friends. She spun out, kicking a wake of dirt in Vlad's face. Halfway back across the pit, she saw Steve and Todd dragging Clark. She headed for them.

(Pick them up. Then drive out of here. Leave that piece-of-shit vampire-wanna-be at the mercy of the nighttime desert.)

She slowed. Vlad stood with his feet wide apart and arms out at his side. The truck levitated. Once the tires left the earth, the diesel engine revved. Dallas felt something wrong with the truck. The headlights tipped her off. They rose until they no longer lit the ground. She couldn't tell how high the truck floated. Her forward momentum stalled. Then it shifted as Vlad pulled her back toward him.

(It's metal.)

Dallas popped the door handle and jumped out of the truck. She fell at least a dozen feet. Since no one had ever taught her how to roll into a fall, she landed awkwardly. She twisted her left ankle and tweaked her knee. More than halfway across the pit, closer to her friends than to Vlad, she made a hobbled run for them. They clustered together and waited for her to rescue them.

(What can I do? No weapon. No vehicle.)

Dallas huffed and puffed as she ran. She turned to look back, expecting Vlad to hurl the truck at the back of her head. But instead, he sat it down and climbed inside. Dallas picked up her pace, expecting him to drive after her.

(He can only control metal.)

She limped hard. Her leg screamed in pain, but she ran for her life. Her heart felt like it would beat out of her chest. And then Vlad puzzled everyone. He turned toward the berm and dug his way out of the pit with his truck. The wheels spun and kicked as he climbed to the top. He sped away, leaving them all behind. Dallas gazed up at the stars in the sky.

(Why did he spare us?)

When no answers came, she stared down at her feet in despair. She spotted Vlad's pipe in the dirt. She snatched it and blew off the dust. Warmth radiated from the brier. She looked in the bowl. No tobacco. No fire. She shoved the pipe in her left, front pocket and limped over to her friends.

And then the strangest thing happened. Her pain disappeared.

18

Power Pipe

The sun rose, and Dallas woke first. Exhaustion overwhelmed her last night, but this morning after only six hours of sleep, she felt refreshed. Feeling no pain, not even her usual morning stiffness, she ran her fingertips over the same leather outfit that she wore yesterday. She wiggled her toes inside the same boots. Dallas rolled out of bed expecting shooting pains and aching joints, but much to her surprise felt neither. Energy surged through her.

(I feel great. Wait. Why?)

The bulge in her left pocket reminded her.

(Vlad's pipe.)

She pulled it out of her pants and examined the carved details of the ebony wood. The remarkable craftsmanship had a somewhat crude quality as if the tools used to carve the pipe were antique.

(Like Daddy's hammer.)

Yet despite the rustic look of the piece, delicate and artful details emerged the longer she gazed at it. The brier felt warm and otherworldly. But it didn't morph and hypnotize her the way it did when Vlad smoked it. She tossed the pipe onto the bedspread.

(Whatever. It's just a pipe.)

Dallas cruised to the bathroom, flicked on the lights, and took a hard look at herself. No limp. No pain.

(I swear I tweaked my leg falling from the truck.)

She splashed cold water on her face and buried her head in a towel.

(Wait. My cheek.)

Tossing her towel aside, she shoved her face as close to the mirror as possible. The whip-slash on her cheek had disappeared too. She traced the spot with her finger tip. The dark skin on her face looked flawless.

(I know I got cut. I saw the blood. On Clark's chainmail. In the rearview.)

She shook it off. "Ugh, this hair," Dallas said, finger combing a wadded mess. Fistfuls had been broken off or torn out. Poking at her relaxed and butchered hair, she felt sad. Discovering a few bald patches made the decision easy.

"Fuck it," she said to herself in the mirror.

Digging under the sink, she found Bella's clippers. The pink electric shearers had only been used once when she buzzed off all her puppy's tufts after she got stuck in a glue trap.

(If it gets in the way, it's got to go.)

Inhaling deeply, Dallas smelled the essence of Bella mixed with the scent of clipper oil. She snapped on a plastic guide comb with the number four embedded in it. Dallas plugged in the shearers, slid the power switch, and listened to the hum.

Buzzzzzzz.

Gazing at herself in the mirror along with a deep, cleansing breath, she recorded a memory. Dallas raised the clippers to her forehead and buzzed a stripe through her hair. Eight-inch over-processed locks fell into the sink. Each pass got easier and faster. And in a minute, her hair disappeared. Switching off the shearers, Dallas pondered the pile of precious hair. Her crowning glory. Now garbage. It laid in the sink, on the counter, and the floor—discarded. She rubbed her palms over her scalp. The sensation.

(Thrilling.)

Dallas perched her hands on her hips. Her hair, her outfit, her fixator; she looked fierce.

(I feel fierce.)

She wrapped her photographic memory of this moment in a feeling of complete freedom.

(I AM fierce.)

When she turned, she found the original *Three Amigos* standing in the doorway, watching her. With both eyes blackened and a bent and swollen nose, Clark stood in his boxer shorts and an R2-D2 T-shirt.

"We had to de-armor your unconscious ass to fit you into the Fiesta last night," Dallas said.

"Sure sounds like a Fiesta," Clark joked.

"Not a party," Steve said, still wearing his camouflage tactical gear.

Todd's battered face and bruised arms looked painful. "Shut up guys. Look at her!" Todd darted into the bathroom and rubbed her little afro, "Fuzzy."

Dallas swatted his hand away, "God dammit, Todd."

"I like it," Clark said, popping Vlad's pipe into his mouth and posing like a corny, Sherlock Holmes.

"Me too," Dallas agreed. Then she saw something amazing. "What's happening?" She pointed at Clark's face.

They gazed at Clark. The black and blue slowly receded from the shrinking bags under his eyes. The swelling decreased. His healthy color returned.

(That pipe.)

"Whoa," Todd said.

As his nose straightened itself, cartilage ground and reset inside. In a few seconds, his face had healed, right before their eyes.

"Hey, my headache's gone," Clark cracked a joke.

"It's that pipe," Dallas said.

"What?" Steve asked her.

"That pipe. I think it heals people."

"That's crazy," Steve said.

"What did you just see?" Dallas asked.

"Gimme that," Todd said grabbing the pipe out of Clark's mouth and sucking on it. Todd dashed in front of the bathroom mirror to watch.

Everyone gathered around Todd. All his bruises faded and disappeared. His lumps shrank, like Clark, the pipe healed him.

"I feel great." Todd passed the pipe to Dallas. "It's magic."

"Pfft, there's no such thing as magic," Clark said.

Dallas touched the bowl of the pipe to her fixator pins, focusing on the near amputation site above her wrist.

"It healed your nose," Steve said.

"There must be some scientific explanation," Clark said. "Let me take a look at that thing."

"Does it matter?" Dallas refused, rubbing the pipe all over her arm. "It works. Don't you dare touch it. I know you. You'll take it apart."

"So," Clark said.

"You might break it."

"Break a pipe? Come on, Mack. I'm an engineer."

Dallas raised her pipe-healed arm into a shaft of light shining through a tiny bathroom window. She twisted the fixator for them to see. Sun glistened off the impressive hardware. "You know what guys? I've got an idea."

19

∩

Percy Plasma

Dallas drove herself to work for the first time in over a month. When she pulled into the employee parking lot of Hoover Dam in her 1960 drab-green Land Rover, Clark and Steve stopped dead in their tracks to stare. She parked, and they ran up to the impressive behemoth of a vehicle.

"Shit, Mack. You *didn't!*" Clark said, impressed as he leaned into the open cabin of the topless vehicle.

"I sure as hell did," Dallas said as she dropped the stick shift out of gear and revved the engine. She let up on the gas. "Take note, Steve. This has a BOP 215, now that's a turbo engine."

"It sure *IS*," Clark agreed as he eyed the interior. "Nice outfit too," he added as he tugged on the bright green fleece jacket with a cut off right arm.

"I had to fit this thing through somehow." Dallas wagged her fixator. "Even though the bone's healed, I'm still sleeve challenged until the surgeons remove this rig."

Enamored with her vehicle, Clark changed the topic, "Two hundred and fifteen horses in a compact aluminum V-8. Mack, I think I love you."

"Isn't it a bit cold to be driving a convertible? It's almost Christmas," Steve asked.

"And you bought right-handed too," Clark said, ignoring his friend's attempt to rain on Mack's parade. "Wait a second." Clark stepped back to get a wide view and examine the big picture. "Is this a Percy? A genuine XOMD Ministry of Defense Royal Air Force truck?"

"Damn right, it is." Dallas smiled.

"How on earth did you find one of these in Vegas?" Clark asked.

"I've got skills."

"I've been driving your ass around for a month, so you could take your time to shop for a British mil-spec off-road truck?" Steve said. "You couldn't just drive down Sahara Avenue and buy a car off the lot like everyone else in Vegas?"

"What can I say? I'm a purist," Dallas smiled as she spun the key and yanked it from the ignition with her left hand. She wagged her fixator in the air, "I still can't shift gears with this. It all worked out when I found this UK import for sale online." She hopped out the right side of the car and slammed the door shut. It made a satisfying, deep sound.

CaCHUNK.

"That's the sound of a solid metal body," Dallas said with pride.

"This is some piece of machinery, Mack." Clark's eyes widened as he touched the hood. "I'm all kinds of impressed."

"Good," Dallas teased.

"It looks like a shoebox without a lid."

"Shut it, Steve," Clark scolded.

"But wait, there's more." Dallas skipped to the open-topped back where boxy bench seats lined the wheel wells. She leaned over the tailgate and reemerged with an overstuffed green leather backpack. The weight of what ever she stashed inside made the straps stretch. As she lifted the pack out of the back of her car, a Teflon weave coated hose dangled from the inside. At the end, a compact plasma cutter hung loose. Dallas threaded her fixator through a strap and swung the pack over her back. She wiggled her other arm to secure the bag. "You're going to shit yourself, when you see this, Clark."

Steve yawned and leaned up against the side of the Land Rover.

Fascinated, Clark had already followed her to the tailgate. He handed her the dangling plasma cutter. When she reached across her body with her good hand to take it from him, Clark's jaw dropped open, "Holy shit, Mack! I think I see where you're going with this."

Dallas twisted two wing nuts and flipped open a pair of gasket clamps. She had welded one to the outside of each of the circular armatures of her fixator. She snapped the handle of the plasma cutter into the gasket, wrenched it down and twisted it shut. She pulled three pairs of round-eye goggles out of a toolbox in the back of her truck. Dallas and Clark slipped on the steampunk safety gear.

Steve shoed the third pair away. "I don't need or want eye protection. I'm not looking anyway."

Dallas shrugged.

"I knew it was just a matter of time before you came up with something," Clark said.

"I always do. Get that, would you?" Dallas pointed at the power box in her backpack.

"My pleasure." Clark reached in and pressed the red button.

The plasma cutter ignited. A six-inch-long ultraviolet flame shot out over her wrist. She pointed the torch in the air, then swished the flame like Zorro. A huge *Z* left a red afterimage on their retinas.

"You're like a superhero now, Mack," Clark said. "I can't stand it."

"Pfft, can we go clock in now?" Steve yawned.

"What's *with* you today?" Clark asked.

"Something's missing. Someone. Hey, where's Todd?" Dallas asked while gesturing to Clark to switch off her plasma cutter. He pushed the red button behind her again and the flame on her wrist disappeared.

"Home sick," Steve said, without looking up.

"Stomach bug," Clark said.

"Ahem!" Steve said pointing at his iWatch.

"Damn, Steve," Dallas said.

"Go on without us!" Clark snapped.

Steve trudged away. Dallas palmed a big pole wedged into her tailgate. The spike was so long that she had to slide it into the Percy diagonally. The fat end crammed into the back corner and ran over the center of the front seat. The spike crossed the passenger side until the tip rested on the top corner of the SUV'S windshield.

Clark shrugged. "What's that?"

"This—" Dallas lifted the end and slid the pole out. "This is what—" She used both hands to heave the pole end in the air, then she let the blunt end of the wrought iron rod drop onto the concrete by her boots. "That motherfucker, Vlad, used to kill Ramone."

"How'd you get that?"

Dallas saluted Clark with her cool and now dormant plasma cutter. Then she raised her eyebrows.

"Okay, gotcha. Plasma cutter. But why on earth would you bring that horrible spike here? To work?"

"I've got a plan, Clark."

"Music to my ears, Mack. Music to my ears."

20

War Hammer

"Show me what you're thinking, Mack."

Clark kicked the mechanic's cage door wide open, then stepped aside to let her pass. Dallas marched in holding her wrought iron spear like a javelin while resting the weight on her left shoulder. Once inside, she let the long pole roll down her arm and fall to the floor. The ends bounced alternatively and settled onto the concrete.

Clang, bong, clang, cling, ting.

Dropping the spear made a hell of a racket, but Dallas didn't care. "That," she said as she pointed to her 165 pound Peddinghaus blacksmith's anvil. In the corner, it sat securely mounted onto an open-box rig she custom welded for it. "We're going to use that. We'll dismantle it and set it free."

"For what, exactly?" Clark asked.

"Wait and see. You better goggle up." She adjusted her eyewear.

Clark found his still strapped across his forehead. He secured them over his eyes. "We need some tunes. How about Daft Punk?"

"Who?"

"Oh my god, Mack. Are you telling me you don't know Daft Punk?"

She shrugged.

Clark dashed over to the workbench and pulled a dust encrusted CD portfolio out from a shelf underneath. He paged through a few sleeves and pulled out a disc with Daft Punk and *Human After All* scribbled on it with black Sharpie. When he went to load it into the boom box, he hit a snag. "Hey? Where's the radio?"

"I trashed it." She pointed at the can.

"Why?"

"It's busted."

Clark retrieved the dusty boom box and plugged it in. He powered it up. The red LED lights glowed, and he swapped out his home burnt disc for the manufactured Stevie Wonder one inside. Then he carefully put her CD into the empty sleeve. "You're gonna love this, Mack." He selected the ninth track. The song *Technologic* blasted from the speakers.

"Not busted," Clark yelled as his eyes lit up with excitement.

"It sounds like robots."

"I know. Isn't it wonderful?" He smiled.

Dallas watched him. His joy burned a beautiful memory into her mind.

(Such honesty. Infectious.)

She smiled. She liked him. Genuinely liked him. She waved him over and gestured to her backpack. "Get over here and help me. We've got a war hammer to build."

Clark came to her aid. "May I suggest something?"

"Sure."

He reached out to help remove her backpack like a butler would removed a guest's overcoat. Holding the

146

green straps of her back pack, Dallas pulled her arms out. Her fixator still tethered, Clark carefully spun her so they faced each other. He threaded her fixator through the strap and let her push her good arm through the other. The backpack hung in front. Clark ducked around and snapped the waist belt in the back and removed the slack.

(I'm impressed.)

"You. You and your brain, Clark." Dallas could reach under the flap and turn her plasma cutter on and off all by herself now. She fired it up. The flame lit over her wrist.

"As impressive as the first time. It's—I don't know. It's spellbinding," Clark said in a trance.

"Are you going to stand there yapping? Or are you going to give me a hand?" Dallas swung a three-step stool next to and anvil. She stepped up. Then she leaned to cut a cylinder through the center of the anvil.

The two worked together, solving problems and building something new. They cut. They hammered. They welded. They supported each other. They helped each other. They took turns leading. They bounced ideas off the other. And most of all, they had fun. Time flew by. Before they knew it, hours had passed.

They stepped back and removed their safety gear. Dallas ran her fixator hand through her fuzzy hair. She felt accomplished. Clark put all the tools and materials away carefully and then stood by her side to admire their creation.

"Now that's bad ass," Clark said.

Stretched out on the floor in front of them, the seven-foot tall war hammer looked like something out of a video game. It reminded Clark of something Todd fabricated in Fallout 4 a few months ago. They had ground the thinest end of the spire into a sharp spike. They smoothed the widest end of the spire into a blunt end. To prevent the head from snapping off on impact, they wedged the thickest diameter through the hammer head. The top stuck out eight inches from the hammer-head anvil. One side had a conical spike, great for piercing. And the other had a triangular striking wedge that reminded Dallas of her father's homemade blacksmith hammer.

"That oughta stop the motherfucker," Dallas said with pride as she bent down to grab the handle. When she went to lift the stellar hammer, the head wouldn't budge. She tried with two hands. She could barely lift the handle off the ground, let alone the anvil. "Uh, I think we might have overlooked a fatal design flaw."

Clark stepped in to help her. Together, all they could do was lift the handle and watch the hammerhead rotate about twenty degrees before it snapped back against the ground.

CLANG!

"Shit," Clark said as he dashed to the boombox and shut off his music.

Silver walked in on them. "Where have you guys been all morning?" He saw the mess and bizarre build on the floor. "What's that supposed to be?"

"Double shit," Clark said, making eye contact with Dallas.

The two engineers froze to await the fallout. Silver shuffled up next to them.

"What is this for?" Silver asked, touching the sharp end of the hammer head. "It looks like a medieval fantasy melee weapon."

"It *does*. Doesn't it?" Clark smiled with pride.

Dallas elbowed him in the ribs. "You wouldn't believe me if I told you, Sil."

"Why don't you try me?" Silver said, losing his patience.

"Look. I'm sorry. I know we're both on the clock, but don't yell at Clark. This was all my idea. We'd get the thing out of here, but we can't." Dallas expected trouble.

"Because it's too heavy," Silver said.

"Right, boss," Clark said. "It's gotta weigh at least 200 pounds."

"Congratulations. Looks like you built a two-hundred-pound, seven-foot war hammer that can't be swung by any human being," Silver said.

The engineers looked embarrassed.

"Well, today's your lucky day, guys," their boss said with a smile. "I'm the one person who can help you."

21

∩

Silver Secret

The three engineers stood around the giant war hammer and stared down at it. Silver gestured and said, "Stand back."

Dallas and Clark took four steps back and leaned against the workbench. Clark gave her a look, and she nodded.

(What the hell is Silver up to?)

They both wondered. Finding each other on the same page more and more, Dallas and Clark no longer needed words to communicate. Silver took a wide stance and spread his arms high. His pudgy body stretched out like a swollen letter *X*. Then he flexed, but muscular limitations made that almost undetectable. His limbs trembled. His face turned beat-red. Seconds passed. Nothing happened.

Dallas gave a *get-a-load-of-this-shit* look to Clark. He smiled, silently agreeing.

(He knows.)

Then suddenly, the war hammer vibrated. It quivered. And then it lifted. It rose a foot off the ground and hovered there.

"Whoa! That's some *Empire Strikes Back* jedi master Yoda lifting Luke's x-wing fighter with the Force shit right there," Clark said as he lunged forward to get a closer look.

Dallas hung back, speechless.

(No words.)

Silver lowered his arms, and the war hammer came to a gentle landing on the concrete. "I prefer *Star Trek*," Silver said, slightly out of breath.

Dallas stepped forward to cut through the shit. "Can we table the science fiction fanboy debate and talk about what just fucking happened here?"

The men raised eyebrows at each other.

"The woman has a way with words," Clark said.

"Well, I lifted it."

"No shit, Sil," Dallas said kicking her steel toe against the boulder of an anvil. It didn't budge. "Let's discuss *how* you lifted it."

"I'm with her," Clark added. "Discuss."

"We have seventeen turbines down here in the plant. Nine on the Arizona wing. And eight here on the Nevada side," Silver explained.

"Yes, Sil. We know this," Dallas said. "Let's skip to the part we don't know."

"Patience, girl. Geesh," Silver said, then he turned to address Clark man-to-man instead.

(Did he just call me 'girl?')

"I've worked down here my entire adult life. Twenty-four years now. And well. Sixteen years ago, right after the birth of my son, I noticed I could move things. With my mind—"

(Bullshit.)

"One day I moved a screwdriver just by thinking about it. I was working in a turbine, and my tools were out of reach. I didn't want to climb out of my spot. I stretched for

151

it." Silver held out his open hand. "And I thought 'if only I were a few inches closer.' And *wham!* The screwdriver shot into my hand." His fingers curled, and his hand closed. Silver continued, "I spent the next decade and a half studying this phenomenon. For the best I can tell, it's some kind of magnetic transference."

(Magnetic transference? Ha!)

"Magnetic?" Clark perked up.

"Maybe you have a lot of iron in your blood," Dallas joked.

The men ignored her.

"'Magnetic transference?' Tell me more," Clark said.

"I've watched our engineers over the years. Trying to figure out if it's just me, or it happens to other people."

"And?" Clark asked, hopeful.

"It's always just been me," Silver said. "Well, until six years ago." He looked at Dallas.

She blushed. She wondered if they could tell she felt ashamed. Then she acted like she didn't know what Silver meant, "What?"

"Dallas, you have this gift too," Silver said.

"Get the fuck out," Dallas said.

"No. You do," Silver insisted.

Then a whole flurry of visual memories flooded her at once. Bella's levitating dog tags. The kitchen knives all pointing at her on the floor. The finial from Ramone's skewer sticking to her fixator. Her fixator sticking to the caboose control panel. Her fixator sticking to Vlad's coffin. Her fixator sticking to the tailgate of Vlad's truck. Over and over again. Her fixator sticking to–metal. She held it out in front of her to examine it more closely in the light.

(My fixator.)

"Is it this thing?"

"No," Silver answered flatly.

"But it's gotten. Stronger since I broke my arm," Dallas said, touching the fixator and fiddling with her customizations.

"It's not that," Silver insisted.

"No. It has to be. I mean a few little odd things happened here or there. But ever since the accident, this thing has been sticking to every damn metal thing in the world. Especially when I'm–" Dallas made an *oh-my-god* face. "Upset."

Silver closed his eyes and nodded knowingly.

"Are you saying that when Mack gets pissed off, she turns into a magnet?" Clark asked.

"For the most part," Silver nodded.

(Not angry. Anxious.)

"But I've always gotten pissed off. And nothing magnet crazy happened until I got this thing." Dallas wiggled the fixator under his face.

"I'm telling you. That's not it."

"Then what *is* it?" Dallas paced circles around the war hammer, thinking out loud, "Ever since the accident." She hoofed laps around the men. "That day you wrote me up." She felt herself getting angry. "Wait! No way. That day you –"

(Broke up with me.)

She glared at Silver. Something else clicked in her mind.

(Ever since we stopped fucking.)

"I'm magnetized. I am." Dallas walked circles in the mechanic's cage. Fast circles, but her brain moved faster.

"Clark, remember what you showed me at *Cafe Coronado?* Remember how you magnetized that butter knife, by rubbing a magnet over it over and over?"

"Yeah, sure I remember."

"Can you demagnetize something by rubbing a magnet over it over and over?"

"Well sure. That's how it works. Lining up electrons. Or scattering them."

"Motherfucker." Dallas poked her index finger into Silver's chest.

(He's been fucking my power away.)

"You," She looked down at his crotch, then back in his eyes. "You've been demagnetizing me for years."

Beads of sweat formed on his pinkening forehead as he stuttered, "Um. Well. Yes. T-t-technically."

"Fucker!"

"But, Dallas. I also demagnetized myself by having relations—" Silver's eyes darted at Clark. He didn't want to say.

"Forget it, Sil. He knows. Everyone knows we were fucking."

"What? How?" Silver poured sweat now. Dark circles spread under his arms. "Did you tell?"

"No. Who cares. Let's get back on topic," Dallas said.

"It's a huge burden to carry around, this magnetism. It causes problems. All kinds of problems," Silver said.

"You don't say?" Dallas glared at him hard.

"It's what drew me to you. And I always felt better after we—"

"Did you ever stop to think. Maybe I should tell her what's going on? Maybe I should give her a fucking choice? You know, like maybe I didn't *want* to be demagnetized by you," her voice grew in volume and force. A rage grew inside her. She got so angry that she saw red. Then she saw blazing white. Her mind lost the ability to record the memorable scene. The colors blurred into the most intense heat she'd ever felt. She felt it through her whole body. Her soul. On fire. The war hammer shot up into the air and flew directly toward her. Without looking, she reached out. She caught it with her fixator hand easily.

"Holy shit, Mack!" Clark said. "You really are a superhero!"

"I'm a goddamn warrior!" Dallas slammed her war hammer through the anvil box-frame like a sledge.

KABLAM!

The box smashed into a hundred pieces.

Silver shrunk into a quivering shell. He camouflaged his fear with a joke, "Yeah, better not piss *that* girl off."

Dallas shot him a nasty look. "Woman."

Silver whimpered out loud. If he were a dog, his tail would have dipped between his legs. He retreated into the opposite corner.

Clark walked over to the workbench and squinted hard at her blacksmith hammer. "Quick, Mack, say something to piss me off."

Instantly, Dallas relaxed when he spoke, yet maintained control over her war hammer. "*Star Wars* sucks."

Clark pointed his fingers at the little hammer like some amateur mentalist. Nothing happened. "Say something else. Hurry."

"And CGI is superior to practical special effects."

"Ew, you sure know how to get to me, Mack." Clark concentrated and gritted his teeth.

Still nothing happened. The hammer stayed perfectly still in front of him.

"More! Make me mad," Clark begged. "Errrr. Rawr." Clark attempted to summon the darkest feeling. He failed.

"Magnets are worthless."

"Not to *me!*" Clark's palms slammed onto the bench, and he steadied himself. "Don't say that, Mack." Clark looked more hurt than angry. "Promise, you'll never say that ever again."

The hammer still did nothing. Dallas's heart, however, melted.

"Maybe you just don't get angry, Clark," Dallas said. "I think maybe, that's great."

"But I want to be a magnet like you." Clark's chin fell into his chest.

Once Dallas knew she had this power, somehow she controlled it effortlessly. When she saw Clark's disappointment, she couldn't stay angry. Not for one more second. He possessed a childlike enthusiasm, yet the stability and ageless wisdom of a real man. A good man.

(And his honesty. I've never known anyone so fearlessly honest before.)

"I want to be a magnet."

Dallas went to him, carrying her two-hundred-pound war hammer with her once broken arm. She put her other hand on his slumped shoulder to encourage him. "I know you do. I know."

"If I can't be a magnet myself. Can I be near *you*, then?" Clark asked looking into her eyes with such sincerity she nearly cried.

"Yes, Clark," she whispered. "A million times, yes."

22

∩

Barrier Breach

Under the cover of darkness, *The Amigos* parked the Percy on the hillside above the caboose of the *Pick-A-Part*. They wore fighting gear and carried their weapons. Dallas stashed her war hammer in the back of the open topped SUV. Steve and Todd propped their feet up on the anvil. On this stakeout, considering the way Vlad ambushed them at the pit, they felt it best to be armed and ready. In the enemy's domain, anything could happen.

"See anything?" Dallas asked as she fiddled with her plasma cutter fixator.

"Nope," Clark said looking through night-vision binoculars with the visor up on his suit of armor.

(What?)

"Are you saying 'Nope' or 'Yup?'" Dallas asked. "I can't tell."

"Nope."

"Is that a 'no'?" Dallas got annoyed.

"Nope."

"Are you saying you saw something?" Dallas couldn't read his expression with the binoculars hiding his face.

"Nope." Clark surveyed the scene.

"What the hell, Clark? Just say 'yes' or 'no!'" Dallas tried not to raise her voice in frustration.

"Jesus, will you two just fuck and get it over with?" Steve commented from the backseat.

"Nope and nope," Clark teased.

"Fuck you both," Dallas teased back. "Give me those." She snatched the binoculars away from Clark. Dallas scanned the junkyard below. The binoculars amplified ambient light and provided an image in all green. Nothing moved in the yard. Dallas pointed to the red train car. "I bet he's been hiding out in the caboose."

"You look funny with goggles on your forehead and binoculars over your eyes. Like an alien insect or something." Clark smiled.

"Why are we here again?" Steve asked from the back seat. "Last time, this guy nearly killed all of us. If he murdered his wife, and he's down there, why don't we just rat him out to Metro?"

"Yeah, let the cops handle it," Todd said.

"Because there's no justice in the world, Steve," Dallas said.

"Cynical much?" Steve asked.

"Fuck the police. We do this my way," Dallas said, still observing through the binoculars.

"Yeah, fuck the Five-O," Todd tried to sound gangster.

"God dammit, Todd." Dallas shook her head. "So I have a theory."

"Do tell," Clark said, leaning in to listen through his helmet.

"You all know how I'm magnetic?" Dallas put down her binoculars and looked around at all her friends. "Before I knew my power, weird shit would happen to metal if I got anxious. But now that I know, I can control it. I don't know why."

"I've been working on the turbines longer than you," Clark said. "I don't understand why I'm not magnetic too."

"I don't know. It's random or something. But Silver knew I was a magnet. He knew before I did. That's why he—" Dallas paused to choose the most sensitive words possible for Clark, "felt attracted to me."

Clark's smile shrank.

Dallas cued up the video on her phone. "Look at this. I know it's for shit. But I saw it when it happened. Vlad controlled that cross. That nickel crucifix. He moved it with his mind. And the swords of the ceiling fan. Same thing."

The Amigos lean in to review the video.

"I can't see shit," Todd said.

"You think he's magnetic too," Steve said.

"Shit. Everyone gets to be a magnet but me. Even the bad guy," Clark said. "I'm going to start sleeping on the turbines. All night. I live there now. Yup. Until I become a magnet too."

"And that's how he attacked us in the pit," Todd said.

"He stops bullets with magnetism?" Steve asked touching the handle of his pistol.

"Like on *MythBusters*," Clark said. "He's got to have one helluva magnetic field to do that."

Dallas put her phone away. "Right, he's way stronger than Silver. Way stronger than me too. I don't know if I can beat him." She raised her binoculars. "I want to go in there. I need to see if I can learn more about this power."

"Wouldn't it be safer to ask Silver?" Steve asked.

"Fuck him. I'm done with him," Dallas said.

159

"So you'd rather face a serial murderer who has already tried to kill you than your X-boyfriend?" Steve asked. "And we're stupid enough to go along with this?"

"Shut it, Steve." Clark said.

"I think Vlad is targeting me the same way Silver did. He knows. He senses the magnetism in me. He knows about my power. And he's drawn to me like—"

"An opposite pole," Clark said.

"You get me." Dallas smiled. "I have to stop Vlad. He'll keep coming after me unless we stop him first," Dallas said. Then she spotted motion inside the caboose. "Hey, something's moving down there."

Everyone leaned forward to look, the almost full moon and the street lamps lit up the scene decently without the aid of night vision. They were too far away to see details, though.

Dallas pointed. "Look. He's leaving."

They watched. A dark figure wearing a black hoodie exited the caboose and hiked toward a taxi cab that was pulling into the entrance way. The shadow jumped into the back seat. And then the cab pulled a U-turn before driving away.

"Okay fearless leader, now what?" Clark asked Dallas.

Dallas patted her backpack that hung across her chest and jumped out from behind the wheel. "Now we go in."

The Amigos followed her lead.

"Are you bringing this thing?" Todd asked pointing at the war hammer.

"Hey, Mack, what kind of range do you think you got?"

Dallas knew exactly what Clark meant and smiled knowingly at him. She stood at the tailgate of her classic Range Rover and easily levitated the massive war hammer with her fixator arm. She glided it over her friends' heads.

Clark gazed in awe as it passed. Steve ducked and dashed out of the way. And Todd reacted like a cat that heard a loud noise.

"I don't care what Silver says. This thing makes it stronger," Dallas said brandishing her fixator at Clark. She hovered the war hammer at a safe distance and walked toward the caboose. After a hundred feet, the war hammer quivered and sank like a cold balloon losing helium.

"That's not bad, Mack," Clark said running up to her. His metal feet clanked against the rocky desert soil. His armor rattled.

Dallas thrust her palm toward her suspended weapon. It immediately reacted and flew into her hand. She gripped it even though she didn't need to, because she liked the feeling of the wrought iron in her hand. "You sound like a running storm trooper."

"I do? Awesome."

"Why on earth did you wear the armor again, Clark?" Dallas used her colossal war hammer as a walking stick.

Steve and Todd followed, trailing behind. They sensed something happening between the two. *The Amigos* hiked downhill until they reached the ridge along the junkyard. From the edge, a three-foot drop led to the roof of the caboose. Dallas jumped first. Then Clark, who landed in a tap dance of metal on metal.

Clang, stomp, tap, tap, tap.

Steve and Todd followed. *The Amigos* stood on top of the caboose. Dallas lowered her war hammer, leaving it to rest. She went straight for the cupola and slid the tiny lookout window open. She recalled escaping through the same window after Vlad had sexually assaulted her. Clark watched as Dallas climbed through. Her ass got stuck going in, just like it did coming out last time. Clark grabbed her boots and gave her a shove. Dallas straightened her legs and wiggled, letting him push her through. Inch-by-inch she squeezed. Pulling on the seat bolted to the floor inside, she struggled. Her face pointed downward toward the winding stairs.

Then suddenly, Todd popped his head into the stairwell below her and shouted, "Hey Dallas!"

Startled, Dallas would have jumped, but she was stuck, so her reaction was a full-body flinch. She gasped, sucking in air and grabbing at her heart. When she calmed, she exhaled and whispered, "God Dammit, Todd."

"Oh, sorry, Mack. Didn't mean to scare you."

"Where did you come from?" Dallas asked still hanging from the window.

Todd pointed back down the hall. "I climbed down the ladder from the roof. The door was unlocked. So, I walked right in."

"You've got to be fucking kidding me," Dallas said, still trying to wiggle through the window. Her leather pants gripped the aluminum frame.

Steve peeked his head into the tiny staircase that led up to the cupola. "You stuck?"

"Yes." Dallas reached out for him.

Steve pulled both her hands, while Clark pushed both her feet. Dallas sucked in her gut and imagined herself stretching.

(Thinner. Taller.)

Then suddenly, her ass broke free, and she flew through the window. Steve toppled backward, Clark and his armor crashed into the window, and Dallas took a full stair-dive. She landed in a handstand on her fixator that should have hurt. But the pipe had healed, maybe even *overhealed*, her broken arm. Steve and Todd backed down the narrow hallway. Dallas followed, finding Clark standing in the open caboose doorway. The Amigos stood inside the strange bedroom-slash-dining room staring at each other in the dark.

"Okay, we're in," Clark said, tapping his metal finger against his thigh armor.

"Yeah, so now what?" Steve asked. Then he spotted the nudie magazine. He picked it up and thumbed through pages of bare breasts. Then he dove into the bunk head first with his mag. He overshot the mattress and disappeared through the wall beside the bed. First his head, then body, and finally, his legs all dropped out of sight.

"What the fuck?" Dallas gasped as she dove after Steve. Then, much like hanging halfway through the window a few minutes ago, her top-half disappeared, with her ass and legs still on the bed.

"I can't even," Todd said.

Clark jumped in to help, moving like a clunky tin man. He touched the side of her knee, and her leg kicked. Kneeling on the bed, he reached out to touch the wall. It looked like a sheer cloth, not a wall. When he touched the surface, it didn't respond like fabric. Clark flipped up his face shield and eyed the barrier closely. "It appears to be a permeable membrane. A cloaking forcefield," he said. Poking at it, he flinched, expecting pain. Instead, his finger penetrated and disappeared. Then he pulled back and his hand was whole again.

"Whew." Clark stuck his whole head through. He saw Dallas's top half on the other side. "You all right?"

Dallas looked up at Clark's floating head, "I think so. She rolled over and pulled her legs the rest of the way through the barrier. "What the hell happened?"

"I don't know, but it's fascinating. Some sort of cloaking shield. Or maybe it's like the event horizon in *Star Gate*."

"You think we found a wormhole?"

"What the hell are you two babbling about?" Steve asked as he stood and brushed off his night camouflage BDUs.

Dallas surveyed their new surroundings. They stood inside the entrance of what looked like a mine shaft. Her head nearly scraped the carved black rock. If she hadn't buzzed her hair, it would have brushed against the ceiling.

Clark scooted through the barrier. When he stood inside the tunnel, his helmet scraped against the top of the mine shaft. He hunched over slightly and tripped over a track running along the floor. "It's dark in here."

Steve reached in his pocket and pulled out a Zippo lighter. Then he pulled Vlad's pipe out from his cargo pants. He flicked the lighter, lit the pipe, and sucked hard.

"So you smoke now?" Dallas asked.

Steve laughed, "Guess my dirty little secret's out now." He held the zippo in the air and examined the walls like Indiana Jones. He discovered a sconce holding and old torch. "Well, look here," he said with his pipe clenched in his perfect teeth. Steve lit the fuel-doused fabric and handed the flaming torch to Dallas. He flipped the top shut on his Zippo and shoved it back in his pocket.

Todd crawled through the barrier to join the rest of *The Amigos*. He passed Clark, who investigated the permeable barrier. Clark observed Todd's entrance, then poked at the portal again. Dallas pointed the torch toward the gradually descending mine shaft.

"You know we have to go down there," Dallas said, looking at her friends. They nodded unanimously.

23

∩

Junkyard Encore

The Amigos descended the mineshaft with Dallas in front lighting the way. She leaned forward at an extreme angle with the torch over her head. Rattling, Clark hunch-walked behind Dallas to be close to her, but also to protect her. Steve followed next, smoking his pipe with arms outstretched, tracing his fingertips along the cold carved walls. Then being the shortest, Todd didn't need to lean at all.

"How far down do you think it goes?" Dallas asked over her shoulder.

"Let's see. A four percent grade. Let's say five to keep it simple. And we've walked about two hundred feet—" Clark did math in his head.

"Oh my God, it doesn't matter," Steve yelled at him. "We're going downward. We can all feel it."

"I was going to say before I was so rudely interrupted, that we're going into the hillside more than down," Clark finished.

"I bet we're under the Percy." Dallas touched the ceiling.

"Maybe. Assuming that caboose wall was only a camouflaged doorway," Clark said.

Dallas waved the torch at a cobweb obsticle. They burned up and shrank away. It smelled like burnt hair and tobacco smoke. "What else are you thinking?"

"It could have been a portal."

"Oh, come on," Steve moaned.

Todd laughed.

"Why not a portal? Who says we're even in Vegas anymore," Clark said.

"Stupid science fiction," Steve mocked.

Clark stopped dead in his tracks, and while still bent over, turned toward his heckler. "Excuse me. Have you ever seen something like that barrier we passed through to get in here? Have you experienced that phenomenon before? Do you know what it is? Do you know all it can do? Do you have a GPS reading on your phone when there's no cellular signal down here? Have you scientifically tested and disproved my theory?" Clark beat him with rapid fire questions. For the first time all night, Steve backed down. "I didn't think so. So why don't you keep your smart ass comments to yourself?"

Unconsciously, Steve nodded slightly. Dallas couldn't take her eyes off Clark during the exchange.

(Amazing.)

Everyone stayed silent as they decended deeper into the mineshaft. Steve got his phone and checked for a signal. His screen said, "No service," where his bars should have been.

"Hey? Can I borrow that?" Todd asked.

"Where's your phone?"

"Forgot it."

"Fine." Steve handed Todd his unlocked Samsung.

Todd pushed a few buttons and opened up the flashlight. He pointed the light ahead of his feet. "Dark back here."

Looking back to see where the light came from, Dallas tripped, dropped the torch, and tumbled forward into an old mining car. "Umpf. Uh, ow!"

Hearing her in distress, Clark lunged into the darkness toward her voice. "Mack? Are you all right?" His armor crashed into the metal mine cart. The sound of clashing symbols echoed through the cavern.

Crash-ash-ash-ash-ash.

Clark retrieved the dying torch from the wet ground in time to save the glowing embers. He waved it gently through the air, providing enough oxygen to reignite the flame. Then he held the torch over the cart. Sprawled face down with her feet up in the air, Dallas squirmed.

"Hold on, Mack. Let me help you."

Dallas relaxed and took his hand. Using leverage, she flipped over and pulled herself into a sitting position inside the boxy car. They locked eyes. She held onto his hand because she wanted to.

(The way he looks at me. Melts my heart.)

Steve stumbled onto something strange. "Whoa, look at this!" Running into a round chamber ahead of the mine cart, Steve pulled a flashlight from his utility belt. Then he shined it into a production shaft that plummeted straight down. Bolted to the wall, a rusty ladder plunged into the darkness. Todd dashed past, jumped onto the ladder, and dropped six rungs into the darkness.

"Todd," Steve yelled down after him. "Get back up here." He lost sight of his friend. "Yo, Bro. Are you all right down there?" Steve asked.

Minutes passed. No answer. Steve looked back and the bonding couple making goo-goo eyes at each other while still holding hands. Steve shrugged and looked down into the black hole. The ground trembled. A wet sound echoed up from below.

Thwuck.

Dust rained down from cracks in the mineshaft ceiling. Todd shot up like a rocket—a rocket impaled on a seven-foot metal spike. His skewered body flew by Steve's face with two feet of metal sticking out of his skull. Shocked, Steve gasped, dropping his smoking pipe. It disappeared below. At the same time, Todd struck the roof with such velocity that the spike drilled into the rock above. It penetrated so deep that Todd's head made contact with the ceiling. His squashed neck bent forward. His phone dropped at Steve's feet.

"No!" Steve yelled as he jumped away from Todd's corpse. Staring up at his still twitching friend, Steve ducked and reached for his phone. Todd had been recording. The quaking stopped, leaving everyone in shock.

Dallas peeked up at Todd from inside the mine car. She sighed with genuine regret and muttered, "God dammit, Todd."

(Last time I'll ever get to say that.)

Steve played the video. The poor low-light resolution made everything grainy. Several seconds of shadowy footage went by, and then a red glow entered the frame. It grew brighter. A field of tall stakes cast shadows, looking like a spike-pit booby trap. Silhouettes of decapitated heads and impaled bodies scattered through the fields. A strobe light flashed split seconds of gore. Then the footage got shaky and dark, ending with a still shot of Steve's tactical boot.

Clark stood in front of Dallas to protect her. Then suddenly, Vlad flew out of the vertical shaft. Smoking his pipe again, he landed next to Steve who barely had time to react. Vlad swished an arm through the air. Todd's spike slid out of the rock overhead and blasted down through Steve's face. It penetrated his body and emerged from his tail-end before cramming into the rock floor.

Dallas witnessed the entire mess from behind Clark. Inside the mine car, she raised her fixator and concentrated. Clark levitated and fell backward into the car next to her, still holding the flaming torch. Dallas made a big circle in the air over the car then pointed her arm back up the shaft. The rusty wheels of the cart resisted at first, but her power overcame.

Screech, squeak -eek -eek.

The car climbed the track. In moments it sped uphill toward the portal.

(Faster. Faster. Pull. Pull!)

The metal mine car accelerated.

Vlad's shadow soared behind them. Clark pointed the torch out the back of the car. The villain flew through the shaft like Superman.

"Mack, you're going to need to increase the velocity," Clark said.

"What?" Dallas concentrated with her eyes shut.

"Faster, Mack! Faster!"

Dallas pointed to her intended destination, making fast, little circles with her hand. She felt the power flowing through her. The mine car got even faster. Sparks shot from the metal wheels as they scraped the rails. And when Vlad nearly caught them, the car hit the end of the track and came to a screeching halt. At the mercy of momentum, Clark and Dallas flew forward, out of the car, and toward the barrier. They flew through. Back in the caboose, they tumbled off the bed and landed on the floor.

Stunned and amped on adrenaline, Dallas jumped to her feet. Clark struggled to stand in his armor. Dallas helped him up, and they ran for the door as Vlad appeared through the caboose portal. Once outside, Dallas stood tall and raised both her arms high. Her war hammer lifted from its roof perch and flew into her hands.

Vlad appeared on the caboose porch. He stood there, smiling. "Dallas."

"Fuck you, Vlad," Dallas yelled as she swung the hammer in a wide circle, sweeping it in front of her. The anvil hooked Vlad by the knees, swept his legs, and pulled him off the porch.

He fell into the dusty gravel driveway at her boots. Dallas kicked him in the face with her steel toes.

(Because I can!)

Vlad's pipe flew out of his mouth and skipped across the gravel. Dallas pointed, and her arms danced like a conductor in front of an orchestra. She raised her war hammer high above her head. Then she swung it with all the force she could summon. The spiked-end drove straight into his heart and out his back, before sticking in the ground.

"I said I'd stop you, motherfucker," Dallas panted, feeling empowered, exhausted, and satisfied at the same time.

"Come on, Mack. Let's get out of here," Clark said.

Dallas yanked her anvil out of Vlad's body and levitated her hammer over the cliff next to the caboose. She followed Clark up the ladder. They looked down at Vlad, then jumped from the caboose roof to the ridge edge to head back for the Percy. Dallas stepped back to the edge of the cliff to have one final look. She needed to see him dead. Save the image in her memory.

(I DID it. Let it sink in. I'm safe now.)

Having trouble levitating her war hammer, she had to move closer, to the cliff edge. Her magnetic range dropped dramatically in the past few moments. She struggled.

(Almost nothing left. Tired. Exhausted. Drained.)

She looked at Clark almost all the way back to the Range Rover. "We lost two amigos. It's just us," she whispered to herself. Then she turned to lift her war hammer. She had to hold on to it, just to move it now.

(Heavy.)

Vlad twitched.

"What the?" Dallas stared.

The fingers on Vlad's hand spread and his pipe flew into his hand. He clenched it. At that moment, Dallas ran after Clark even though she barely had the energy to move. Slowing down, she drug her hammer behind her. She made it back to Clark, loaded her war hammer into the Percy, and collapsed.

24
U
Pole Switch

Clark drove Dallas back to the dam in her Percy. She slumped to his left barely able to move. Reaching, he checked her seatbelt. Nervous, he tried to keep her awake, because he feared he'd lose her. He wanted to take her to the emergency room. But back when she could still talk, Dallas insisted they go to the dam instead. He engaged in meaningless chit chat to keep her with him.

"This Percy sure handles like a dream," Clark said, keeping his eyes on the road and looking for her response at the same time. "They don't make 'em like this anymore."

"Mmmm," Dallas mumbled, her eyes rolled back in her head.

Clark pressed the gas as they navigated out of the serpentine and over the top of Hoover Dam. Even when trying to speed, he still drove safely. Clark couldn't help himself. Still wearing his suit of armor, he lifted his visor. When he reached the freight entrance on the Arizona side, he greeted security. A husky female officer approached what should have been the driver's side of the Percy. She gave Dallas the once over, then looked at Clark.

"Mack looks bad. You should take her to the hospital," the guard said.

"I know, Rhonda, but she needs to get inside."

She pointed at the green pack across Dallas's chest, "What's with the papoose?"

"Her gear."

"And what's with the getup. Were you at the Ren Fair or something?"

"No. Can you lift the gate?"

"Fine. I'll let your shiny metal ass in." Rhonda reached inside her shack and pushed a button. The long yellow arm of the stop gate swung up into the air.

Clark took off as soon as he had clearance. He drove on the cliffside driveway, thankful for the guardrail. It made him feel safe while seven hundred feet above the Colorado River. He had the Percy under control but tried not to look down. He drove to the oversized freight elevator, popped the stick into neutral, and pulled the parking brake before hopping out. He ran to the control panel and pressed the big green button. Gears whirled. Hustling, he jumped behind the wheel. Then the elevator doors opened horizontally. Clark drove inside. He had plenty of room to open the door and walk around in the elevator. His feet tapped against the industrial metal floor.

Tap, tap, tap, clang, tap.

He pushed the power plant button and waited. He felt his stomach rise as the car dropped. On the slow trip down into the belly of the dam, Clark got behind the wheel again. After a minute, the elevator doors opened.

Ding, ding.

The familiar home-away-from-home of the turbine hall greeted him. He backed out of the elevator, pulled a K-turn, and sped through the east wing.

Dallas bobbed her head and opened her eyes. "We're here?"

"Yes, Mack." Clark parked and helped her out of the Percy to her feet.

Appearing from behind a turbine, Silver shuffle-waddled to them. "What happened to her?"

"We got attacked," Clark said. "We lost Steve and Todd."

"'Lost?' What do you mean, 'lost?'"

"They're dead." Dallas lifted her head.

"Dead? How?"

"Vlad impaled them," Dallas said, her lucidity returning.

"Vlad? Who the hell is that?"

"He's—" Dallas searched for the right words. "He's my neighbor. A vampire."

Uncomfortable with her choice of words, Clark cringed. "He's a bad guy. A real one. Maybe the original one. But we beat him. He's gone."

"Well, that doesn't tell me a damn thing about my two dead employees." Silver pulled out a prescription bottle from the pocket of his khakis. He twisted the cap and popped out a dark green pill the size of a breath mint. "Here, Dal. Take this."

"What is it?" Clark asked.

"An iron supplement," Silver said. "I wish I had some orange juice for you."

"I'm not taking any pill from you." Dallas resisted and got dizzy. She couldn't walk. She had to brace herself on the edge of her Percy to keep from falling down.

"You need it, Dallas. The iron. It will help you," Silver said, holding the pill in his hand.

"Fuck you," Dallas said, bent over her truck.

"I guess now's the time to tell you. I've been slipping you these for years. Usually in your food," Silver said, casting his eyes to the floor.

"What the fuck, Sil?" Dallas wanted to get angry, but didn't have the energy.

"It's only iron," Silver said. "But it helps make your magnetism, stronger."

"That's why you brought me Archie's takeout when you wanted to–" She stopped herself from finishing the sentence. She didn't want to hurt Clark's feelings. "I don't need it. I'm already feeling better now that I'm down here."

"About that, Mack," Clark said.

"Yes, that's part of it too," Silver interrupted. "You need to be near the turbines and loaded with iron. You need both."

Clark took the pill from Silver's hand and helped Dallas stand. She leaned on him for support. He looked her in the eye. "Do you trust me, Mack?"

Dallas gazed at him and said, "Absolutely."

"Then take the pill." Clark offered it to her.

Dallas nodded and opened her mouth. Clark placed the pill on her tongue like a communion wafer. Dallas shut her mouth and dry swallowed the pill.

"Why don't you go fetch her some orange juice?" Clark said looking over his shoulder toward Silver.

Silver waddled toward the break room.

"What's with OJ?" Dallas asked, still leaning on him.

"It's the vitamin C. It helps the iron absorb and bind in your blood cells." Clark propped her up against the Percy.

"How do you know this?"

"My sister's anemic." Clark buckled the waist strap of her back pack and handed her the tethered plasma cutter.

Together they attached it to her fixator. "We need to move, Mack."

"Why, what's wrong?"

"I have a theory," Clark said as he jogged away from her. His feet tapped on the concrete floor.

Clang, clang, clang, tap, tap, clang.

Clark jumped into the forklift, put on his seatbelt, and turned the key. The engine started. He pulled a few levers. He rolled the forks through two bottom support brackets of the cage used to lift engineers into the air for high work. After raising the forks a few inches and backing up, he delivered the cage to Dallas.

"The man bucket?" Dallas opened the cage door.

"People lifter! Get in, Mack," Clark yelled over the idling engine.

Silver returned with a bottle of Tropicana and handed it to Dallas. She thanked him and drank half the juice.

"You got another one of those pills?" Dallas asked.

"Not a good idea. It'll rip up your stomach," Silver said, handing her the bottle.

"I'm not too worried about my tummy right now." Dallas took another pill from the bottle. "Vlad's still alive."

"But how?" Clark asked, astonished. "I saw you kill him."

"That pipe, Clark." Dallas said as she popped another iron pill and chugged the rest of the juice.

Silver took her empty bottle and closed the bucket door for her. Dallas slid the safety pin through the latch and gave Clark the thumbs up. Pulling a few levers, he lifted the cage-box high. He drove her to Turbine No. 8, the newest and most powerful turbine in the hall. Then he set her down as close to the spinning magnets as possible, just off center from the central catwalk.

"So, what's this about, Clark?" Dallas yelled over the noise of the turbine.

"Reversing polarity," Clark yelled back. "You spend what? Almost all of your time outside the turbines, right?"

"Well sure. The only time we're inside a turbine is when it's down," Dallas agreed. "And hey, I'm feeling better already." She smiled.

"That's great, Mack. So, if water spins the magnets of the turbine in the same direction, and you're always standing outside—"

"Then if I stand inside, it should reverse my polarity!" Dallas jumped up and down in the bucket. "You're a goddamn genius, Clark."

"Why thank you, Mack." Clark blushed inside his steel armor.

"I coulda took the catwalk and stood there," Dallas pointed to the center post of the turbine.

"I know, but," Clark paused. "I want you at the exact right spot, and," Clark paused again. "Safe. Safe inside the cage."

"Safe from what?" Dallas asked.

Clark changed the topic. "So while you're drained, we should be able to flip your poles and recharge you. Reversed."

"I get it!" Dallas applauded. Then she stopped and asked with a quizzical look on her face, "But why? Why switch my poles?"

"Because," Clark had to yell for her to hear him, and he really didn't want to yell what he had to say next. "Because your magnetism attracts bad people, Mack."

Dallas stared at him, "what do you mean?"

"I mean, Vlad keeps finding you. You said you think he feels you. Your magnetism. And *that* guy." Clark pointed his thumb toward Silver. "You have so much more to offer than battling dragons all the time."

Tears welled up in her eyes. "Oh, Clark."

"Maybe if we flip your polarity, you'll repel this misery. And attract goodness and beauty instead."

Dallas bawled.

(*I feel healed. Energized. More powerful than ever before.*)

"Don't cry, Mack," Clark said from behind the wheel of the forklift, wishing he could hold her.

25

U

Damn Dam

Ding, ding.

The elevator doors opened again.

"Dallas," Vlad said through his pipe as he stepped out of the elevator. His voice boomed.

"Fuck!" Dallas looked at Clark.

"How are you feeling? Are you up for this?"

(Do I have a choice?)

"I think so." Dallas spun 180 degrees to face her nemesis. "How'd you find me, motherfucker?"

"Secret," Vlad said blowing smoke through an evil grin. He plucked his pipe from his mouth. Then he parted his lips and wagged his fully regrown tongue at her in a vulgar insult. He returned to smoking, moving with smooth, measured steps.

Deciding to stay in the open-top cage, for both protection and an endless supply of power, Dallas pressed the red button in her pack. Her plasma cutter ignited.

Clark gestured at his forehead. "Your goggles."

Remembering, Dallas nodded and pulled her round welding goggles down to protect her eyes. Then she started cutting the cage. She cut through bars and the woven metal grate welded to the inside of the bucket. When she finished, she removed a two-foot square at chest height. She switched off the torch and shoved both her arms through her access space. Dallas reached out, spread her fingers, and her war hammer levitated in the back of her Percy. Then it flew through the air toward her faster than ever, and she caught it easily.

"I thought if we reversed my polarity he wouldn't find me." Dallas looked at Clark.

He shrugged. "It's only a theory. I don't know. I haven't tested it yet."

"Let the testing begin," she said.

Vlad raised one hand in the air and metal tools and turbine pieces next to him, floated and flew through the air toward them. He pelted Silver in the head with a massive crescent wrench. Clark got hit with a ten-pound gear that left a dent in the torso of his armor. Various tools and bits blasted the bucket, but only tiny things like wrench sockets and bolts got through to hit Dallas. They hurt less than hail.

(He'll get pounded.)

Dallas yelled at Clark, "Take off your seatbelt."

"What? Why?" Clark asked getting pummeled by bigger and bigger pieces of turbine.

"Just do it," Dallas yelled.

Clark unbuckled his belt. Dallas held her war hammer in her fixator hand and pointed at Clark with her other one. Clark hovered up out of his seat. Dallas guided him safely out of the forklift and through the air. He levitated above the people lifter. He realized what she intended, so he straightened up tall. She gently lowered him into the cage with her.

"Thanks, Mack."

"A tight fit." She wiggled, still holding her war hammer outside the bucket.

Changing focus, Vlad blasted every piece of loose metal in the turbine hall at Silver. The guy got hit left and right. He tried to swat objects away, but they landed with incredible force. An oversized C-clamp broke Silver's forearm.

He howled in pain. "Dallas, help!"

As metal boxes and shipping crates flew through the air toward Silver, Dallas reached outward, able to slow and deflect their path. Vlad closed in on them. From only a few turbines away, he laughed malevolently. It sent shivers down her spine. Silver crawled, seeking cover behind anything he could find. He chose the Percy. Vlad dropped his arms. He walked with a casual gate as if strolling on the Promenade.

"He's like the Terminator," Clark whispered to Dallas.

Suddenly, Vlad made a grand gesture and lifted the Percy. He pushed it toward the couple suspended by the forklift. Dallas reached out with both hands, pointing her war hammer, using all her power to push back. The two engaged in a magnetic push-of-war, fighting over the hovering SUV between them.

"He's too strong for me."

"Then don't push back," Clark said. "Divert. Go sideways."

Dallas understood and concentrated on a perpendicular vector. The Percy slid off to the side easily. And when it landed closer to her than Vlad, Dallas controlled the vehicle by setting it down safely behind a turbine.

Angered by the defeat, Vlad raised both his hands violently in a push gesture. The Percy flipped over and landed on Silver. The top frame of the windshield, came crashing down on Silver's neck like a guillotine. His head popped off and rolled across the floor. The Percy crushed the rest of his body. Traumatized, Dallas made eye contact with the severed head. It blinked at her. Blood sprayed out from under the Range Rover pulsing with Silver's still beating heart.

(Does his brain realize it's dead yet?)

Her brain did. She processed his death before the blood stopped spraying.

(Dead. Gone. Never going back.)

A crashing rumble interrupted her memory saving process.

BOOM!

She locked eyes with Clark. "That came from outside the dam."

Vlad's rusty pickup truck crashed through a window in the outer dam wall that faced the Colorado River. The same truck from the pit busted a huge hole through the structure and flew toward them. It collided with Turbine No. 8 and shook Dallas and Clark in their bucket.

Seeing the concern in her eyes, Clark reassured her, "Not a load bearing wall."

Dallas swung her massive hammer parallel with the floor and hurled it in Vlad's direction. It spun through the air like a boomerang. She concentrated and pushed with all her effort to increase the hammer's momentum. Vlad refused to change course. He kept walking right for them, smoking all the way. The heaviest, blunt end hit him square in the chest, completely impaling him, like last time at the junkyard.

Except this time, Vlad did not fall. He didn't even slide backward an inch. He kept walking. He kept smoking. He grabbed the war hammer by the handle and pulled it from his chest. He cocked it high above his head.

"He was faking," Dallas gasped.

"What?" Clark asked.

"Back at the junkyard. He was faking. He wasn't hurt." Dallas flexed both her arms through the access hole and pointed them at the Percy. Her muscles tensed, and her body quivered. And with all her strength, she managed to levitate the Percy a few inches off the ground.

Vlad released the war hammer, and it tumbled anvil over handle in their direction. The gaping hole in his chest filled with smoke as he took a deep drag on his pipe. As the hammer closed in, Dallas lifted the Percy to block it. The anvil stuck in the tailgate. Dallas dropped the blood smeared vehicle. It crashed on Silver's corpse a second time.

Vlad's wound healed itself right before their eyes. Smoke morphed into regenerated flesh. "I am immortal!" Vlad's voice boomed.

"We might be fucked, Clark."

"Think positive, Mack," Clark answered as he popped the pin on the latch. "We have to get his pipe." Clark exited the cage. His armor scraped the side of the turbine as he slid down to the floor.

"No!" She started after him.

"You stay safe!" Clark yelled as he ran toward Vlad.

Vlad swept both his arms low to high across his body. Like a wave that emanated, he lifted both the Percy and its embedded war hammer and hurled it into Clark. The force slammed the Tin Man into Turbine No. 7, sandwiching him between two hulking boulders of metal.

"Nooooo! Motherfucker!" Dallas screamed with a rage she didn't know she had. She swept her arms to pull the wreckage off Clark and slammed the Percy into Vlad, purposely hitting him in the face. The pipe tumbled out of his mouth and slid across the floor. This time Dallas kept pushing. She pushed that son-of-a-bitch the entire length of the turbine hall, gathering more and more momentum. She slammed Vlad against the reinforced concrete bunker wall.

Dallas jumped out of the cage and off the side of the turbine. She ran. It was the hardest, most important sprint she'd ever run in her life. She ran for the pipe. A simple fifty-yard dash, but her brain screamed in fear.

(Go! Go! Push! Faster. RUN!)

She pumped her arms and legs. Blood rushed through her. Oxygen filled her lungs. She puffed. She ran. Her pack bounced against her chest. And in less than eight seconds, she got there. She slid into the pipe like it was home base and grabbed it with her good hand.

(Get up!)

Dallas ran again. She sprinted back to Clark. He wheezed, his breathing labored. With his armor smashed into his torso, his lungs couldn't expand inside the tight, crumpled tin can that restricted them. On her knees, Dallas held her fixator hand over his heart. She closed her eyes and concentrated and pulled the dent out of his armor. As the metal popped back into place, Clark's lungs sucked air.

Pop. Op. Clink. Gasp.

Dallas opened her eyes and stared into Clark's.

(Forever.)

She put the lit pipe in his mouth. "I know you can't breathe, but you have to smoke this."

Clark nodded.

"Can you hold it in your lips?" Dallas touched his ear gently.

Clark nodded.

"I've got work to do." Dallas stood to face the mess at the end of the hall.

"Be safe," Clark managed to eek out the words.

"Don't speak. Smoke," she said as she pressed the red button and ignited her plasma cutter. Dallas ran down the turbine hall. Full speed, she closed in on the Percy. She hoped to find a bloody mess when she got there, but she had no idea what to expect.

(Expect gore. But be ready for anything.)

She slowed to a jog and made a swatting motion with one hand. The Percy peeled off the wall and tumbled to the side. A bloody busted up mess of Vlad stuck to the wall. He looked dead.

"Right. But you looked dead before, motherfucker," Dallas said as she made a fist and dropped it away from the torch resting above her fixator. A welding expert, she decided to enjoy the next few minutes.

Smashed, Vlad still stood before her. Taking his fractured jaw in her free hand, she went to work. Dallas cut and dissected. Bit-by-bit, she cut that monster apart. She recorded the memory frame-by-frame. She'd replay this one over and over. The torch cut, she smelled it. Not flesh cooking, but the scent of hot ozone. The torch cut, she heard it. Not sizzling, but the sound of gas escaping. The torch cut, she felt it. Not pain, but the sensation of force weakening. The torch cut, she tasted it. Not blood, but the flavor of iron in her saliva. As the torch cut, she felt herself. Becoming. As she deconstructed reality, as she dismantled fear, her identity solidified.

(Glorious.)

Then all that remained of Vlad was a pile of smoldering bits.

"Immortal, my ass," Dallas said, switching off her plasma torch. She kicked her steel toes through the pile of his ash, scattering Vlad's remains. She wrapped her memory in the feeling of triumph and lifted her goggles to get a clearer view of the world around her.

Smoking the pipe, Clark walked up behind her. "Great job, Mack. Using heat to destroy a magnet. Brilliant."

Dallas blew across the barrel of her plasma torch like it was a smoking gun.

Clark puffed away on the pipe. "You are my favorite person in the whole world."

Dallas turned away from the wreckage, so thrilled to see him healthy and full of life. She threw her arms around him and gave him the biggest hug ever. He wrapped his metal-clad arms around her, careful not to squeeze too hard.

"How are you feeling?" Dallas asked, looking for signs of damage or physical trauma.

"Strong," Clark answered. "How are you feeling?" Clark asked.

"Free," Dallas said taking a deep, cleansing breath.

Dallas used her magnetism to hold Clark in the embrace. When he tried to break from the hug, he couldn't let go. His armored hands stuck to her back. Not that he minded.

Clark laughed, "You got me, Mack."

"I sure do."

THE END

Nevadaland

What could possibly go wrong?

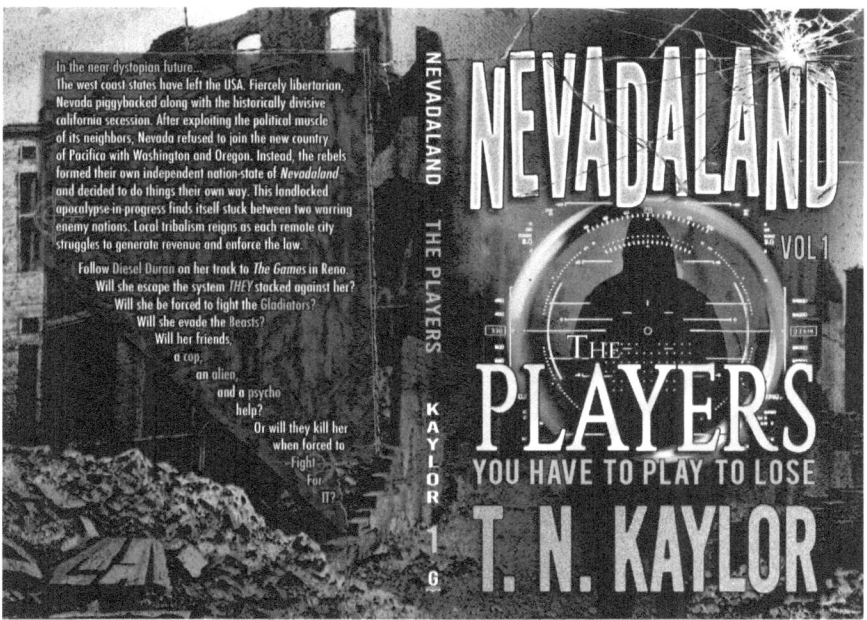

In the near dystopian future...

The west coast states have left the USA. Fiercely libertarian, Nevada piggybacked along with the divisive and historic California secession. After exploiting the political muscle of its neighbors, Nevada refused to join the new country of Pacifica with Washington and Oregon. Instead, the rebels formed their own independent nation-state of *Nevadaland* and decided to do things their own way. This landlocked apocalypse-in-progress finds itself stuck between two warring enemy nations. Local tribalism reigns as each remote city struggles to generate revenue and enforce law.

Follow Diesel Duran on her track to *The Games* in Reno.
Will she evade the mutant beasts?
Will she be forced to fight against the gladiators?
Will she escape the system *THEY* stacked against her?
Will her friends; a cop, an alien, and a psycho help?
Or will *THEY* kill her when forced to fight for it?

NEVADALAND THE PLAYERS

Chapter 1 - The Fast Track

The year 2020. Sixteen years ago.

Inez stomped the gas. The '87 El Camino engine hammered out an angry rebuttal. It lurched forward. It misfired. Eventually, the rusty beast responded in a way that almost satisfied. With his wife next to him on the torn bench seat, they hurled down the deserted highway. On an urgent mission, the solitary vehicle struggled on the sunny Nevada morning. Eloisa groaned in pain and reached down to feel the stickiness between her legs. Without a word, she raised her blood-soaked hand toward Inez. Neither could believe their eyes. And Eloisa couldn't believe how terrifying it felt. Inside.

"You must go faster! Something's wrong. It's bad. *GOD*. It's bad!" she screamed as she held her pregnant stomach and winced in pain.

"It is not time yet." Inez smashed the accelerator to the floor. "We still have two months."

"Tell that to the baby," Eloisa wailed in agony. She panted while resisting the overwhelming need to bear down and push. "Faster. You must go faster!"

Inez forced all his weight onto the gas pedal, crushing it as hard against the floor as possible. As the speedometer crept up a few notches to 103 mph, the Chevy roared and raced westward on I-80. Even while wearing shades, the morning sun blinded Inez as it bounced off the rearview. Squinting, he swatted at the mirror. Green afterimage dots floated over the dash. The tachometer needle pushed into the red warning zone. After four hours trekking across northern Nevada on a hot October day, the temperature needle swept into the red H zone.

"Do not overheat. Now is not the time. Come on. We are almost there," Inez whispered while patting the dash.

They raced out of the salt flats and into the canyon past Lockwood. With no other cars to dodge, Inez maintained his high speed. He rode the dashed center line to avoid the potholes on the outer edge of each lane. The winding Truckee River and Union Pacific railway blurred along the lower side of the divided highway. The valley opened in front of them, revealing a roadblock of Nevada Highway Patrol officers with the Reno skyline waiting behind it.

Inez eased off the gas pedal. Instantly the metal jalopy slowed. Less than a mile away and closing in on the blockade, Inez braked. All four wheels squealed. Irritation. Eventually, the car came to a squeaky stop next to a line of safety cones that reminded Inez of the DUI checkpoints from the days of the Old Republic. But since secession, this independent nation-state of Nevadaland stopped enforcing drug and alcohol laws. That meant no more checkpoints.

Hell, law enforcement had stopped enforcing and prosecuting all misdemeanors as soon as independence ratified. Recently, They passed a new policy to send all suspected felons Fast Track to The Games. These days, cops detained and delivered all the new players. Also, the police served as Nevadaland's only military force, a national guard of sorts, protecting the city perimeter from The Wilds.

"We are wilds," Inez mumbled to himself, concerned.

The couple hadn't been to Reno since Nevadaland declared independence two years ago. On their entire road trip, they hadn't seen a single patrol car on the interstate. Now they idled, facing an entire blockade of dozens of NHP vehicles, fire trucks, ambulances and even a SWAT tank. A police officer strolled up to the driver's window as Inez cranked down the handle frantically.

"Welcome to Reno," the officer said.

"Thank God." Inez leaned out the window.

"God? Well, thank you, my son. Papers?"

"My wife is in labor. Something must be wrong. We need to get to a hospital."

"Slow down there, *Jefe*. No one gets into the city without papers." The cop hid his intentions behind mirrored sunglasses.

"We do not have papers."

"You're both wilds?"

"Yes, sir. We drove in from Battle Mountain. We need help. My wife needs a doctor."

Eloisa moaned and then screamed in pain. She held out both her bloody hands, pleading with the officer.

"No one gets into the city without papers," the policeman repeated, unaffected.

"I will register," Inez volunteered.

"No!" Eloisa objected.

"I have to. I have to get help for you." Inez touched her face with the palm of his hand.

Eloisa cried, "Oh, dear Jesus, no."

"I will register, Officer," Inez said, placing both his hands on the top of the steering wheel to signal compliance.

"Excellent. We're always pleased to recruit a new contestant for The Games." The policeman waved to another. "Pull in over there. That officer will get the process started."

Sobbing, Eloisa, clenched her stomach and wailed.

"Is there any way to expedite this, Officer?" Inez asked, worried for his wife.

"Are you requesting Fast Track?" the officer asked.

"Inez, no! Do not do this. Please. I beg you."

"You will die if I do not."

"You'll die if you do," she said.

"We have no choice. I have to."

"But Inez, you said–" She flinched in pain and shook it off. "You always said–" She glared at the officers eavesdropping. "You know what you said." Eloisa panted. Weak, defeated, and full of worry, she dug around in her cleavage and retrieved a well-worn folded Post-It Note. With trembling hands, she unfolded the pink paper and gave it to her husband.

In blue ball-point pen, the scribbled words read, "You have to play to lose."

Frowning, Inez crumpled up and dropped the note.

191

"But Inez," Eloisa begged. She dove to the floor to retrieve the message he had passed to her at work in the Turquoise Ridge Mine a few years ago. Stabbing pains shot through her entire torso. The cop noticed her sudden move, so she crammed the wadded paper back into her bra before he could see the note.

"Are you requesting Fast Track?" the suspicious patrolman repeated as he pressed a lapel camera button to timestamp this spot of the recording.

"Yes, sir."

"I need you to say the words. I need you to say, 'I, state your name, request Fast Track.'"

"I, Inez Duran, request Fast Track."

"Excellent." The policeman tapped his lapel button again then spoke into the radio on his shoulder, "You heard the man. *Vamonos.*"

Instantly, an ambulance appeared and parked next to the El Camino. Two Medics opened the passenger door and yanked Eloisa out of the pickup. She clawed and fought with what little energy she had left. Blood gushed down her leg and splattered the asphalt. The cop opened the driver's side door, and Inez stepped out. He turned toward his car and placed his hands on the sun-blistered roof of the El Camino. He relaxed. The officer snapped a transparent tubular collar around Inez's neck, then tapped the lock. The compliance collar glowed bright blue. Unable to cope with her grief, Inez tried to mentally filter out the sound of her cries.

Eloisa kicked and slipped out of the paramedic woman's grip. Bleeding and exhausted from the slaughter house between her legs, she limped over to her husband. Eloisa threw her arms around him and buried her face in his chest. All she could do was sob. She needed him to hold her.

"I will fight for you." Inez gazed into her eyes one last time and stroked her long brown hair. "I will fight for both of you." He touched her belly.

"No! Don't go," she begged.

A medic tore her away from her husband.

"That's right. Fight for it," the patrolman said in a satisfied tone. He escorted Inez into the back of a squad car.

The police officer slammed the car door behind Inez. Defeated, Eloisa climbed onto a rolling stretcher, and a paramedic buckled her down and rolled her into the back of an ambulance. The ambulance followed the squad car through the parting road block. They headed west on the highway side-by-side. After a mile or so, the ambulance exited first, taking Eloisa to the emergency room. Later, the squad car exited, taking Inez to The Coliseum.

Neither Inez nor Eloisa would live to see the other ever again. Neither would live to see their child born. And neither would live to see the next sunrise.

About the Author

T. N. Kaylor lives in a "classified" location in Nevada where she weaves an endless parade of colorful characters into macabre tales that keep readers up all night. As a child, timeless reruns of *The Twilight Zone* and *Alfred Hitchcock Presents* served as her black-and-white babysitter. Her early literary influences included Stephen King and Edgar Allan Poe. At age twelve, she wrote her first horror story on wide-ruled notebook paper with a No. 2 pencil. As it circulated, she found the horrified reactions of teachers combined with the squealing delight of her peers to be powerfully addicting.

She has been writing ever since.

Over the course of her career, she has been a technical writer, published academic and copy editor. Now, building on those literary skills, she chooses to inject her dark humor and twisted imagination of the weird, surreal and grotesque into gritty, character driven fiction.

She has published several short stories in weird anthologies and fringe magazines. Catch her award winning short *Death Ray Potato Bake* in *Dark Designs: Tales of Mad Science*. Her print-only collection of word art, *The Zen of Horror*, is now in its forth edition. Her urban horror novella *Magnitude* features a magnetic battle with Vlad the Impaler. And for a dystopian apocalypse-in-progress series, try *Nevadaland 1- The Players* with beasts, robots, and aliens that add an *X-Files* flavor to a dying alternate world.

Currently, she's working on *Nevadaland 2- The Games* and *Nevadaland 3- The Fires*. For a brutal spin on science fiction, look for her dark space novel, *The One*. Join her in this post-modern twilight at tnkaylor.com, if you dare.

Connect on Social Media

www.ingramcontent.com/pod-product-compliance
Lightning Source LLC
Chambersburg PA
CBHW022108170626
46808CB00002B/649